PUFFIN BOOKS

Editor: Kaye Webb

MY THIRD BIG STORY BOOK

Many who read the earliest of Richard Bamberger's story collections, *My First Big Story Book*, when we first published it, and maybe then the second book, will now be ready for this 'older' book of stories, which will delight everyone till the end of childhood.

All the old characters are still here, of course, the princes and princesses, the wicked queens, the witches, and the magic which is almost a character in itself, but most of these stories have some more serious, thoughtful message hidden within them than the happy-go-lucky fables of the earlier books. There's the story of Mayflower, who trod on a golden flower which gave her the power to talk to animals; the beautiful tale of the woodcutter's daughter who searched 'east of the sun and west of the moon' for the faithful husband she had lost by her curiosity, and the one about the princess who laughed at her suitor King Thrushbeard for his looks – and lived to rue the day, as well as more familiar stories like Beauty and the Beast, Dick Whittington, and Hans Andersen's famous *The Snow Queen*.

Richard Bamberger has been President of the International Board on Books for Young People, and is uniquely qualified to compile this collection of stories from many lands.

Richard Bamberger

My Third Big
Story Book

Translated by James Thin

Illustrated by Emanuela Wallenta

Puffin Books

Puffin Books, Penguin Books Ltd,
Harmondsworth, Middlesex, England
Penguin Books, 625 Madison Avenue,
New York, New York 10022, U.S.A.
Penguin Books Australia Ltd, Ringwood,
Victoria, Australia
Penguin Books Canada Ltd, 2801 John Street,
Markham, Ontario, Canada L3R 1B4
Penguin Books (N.Z.) Ltd, 182–190 Wairau Road,
Auckland 10, New Zealand

First published as *Mein drittes grosses Märchenbuch* by
Verlag für Jugend und Volk, Vienna

This translation published by Oliver & Boyd Ltd 1967
Published in Puffin Books 1975
Reprinted 1977, 1978

Made and printed in Great Britain by
Cox & Wyman Ltd, London, Reading and Fakenham
Set in Intertype Baskerville

Contents

Dear Children, Dear Young Friends

Yes, perhaps it is better to address you now as friends, for the third big story-book is intended to accompany you beyond the years of childhood, into adolescence. To begin with, you will find stories which you may have heard already, and which may be quite familiar to you. But then we move on to longer stories, quite different from what has gone before. These stories come from the pens of great writers of many different times and lands, such as Hans Christian Andersen, Oscar Wilde, Wilhelm Hauff and others.

Although these tales have a thread of magic running through them, they deal, nevertheless, with the experiences of everyday life. As in the previous volumes, I am sure you will like the pictures, and I would like to thank the artist for having immersed herself so deeply in the stories that her drawings and pictures are a true reflection of the atmosphere and feelings of the text, as if she were actually living in the stories. I should like to think that you will keep some sheets of paper by you and draw your own pictures as you read. Let your imagination work, and you will have great fun building up your own album of pictures to accompany this book.

It will soon become clear to you from these tales that the art of story-telling goes far beyond a simple tale told to amuse and entertain children. The glittering world of magic, created by a vivid and lively imagination, is interwoven with a profound worldly wisdom and human understanding.

These longer tales have another great gift to offer you: they have many of the qualities of true poetry and great literature, and will lead you on into the wide and fascinating realm of books, which is eagerly sought by everyone who wants more from life than a dull, practical day-by-day existence. I should like to think that a great many of you will find your way into this wonderful magic realm, which exists not merely in dreams and imagination, but between the two covers of a book or the four walls of a library. I wish you joy in your search for it!

RICHARD BAMBERGER

The Seven Foals

There was once a poor man who lived with his wife in a wretched hut deep in the forest, where they barely managed to eke out a meagre existence. They had three sons, of whom the youngest was called Cinders, because he was always rummaging round in the ashes.

One day the eldest son said he wanted to go out and find some work. His parents raised no objection, so off he went to seek his fortune. All day long he journeyed, and when darkness was falling he came to a king's palace. The king happened to be standing on the palace steps, and he called out, 'Whither away, my fine young fellow?'

'I'm looking for work,' replied the lad.

'Will you work for me and look after my seven foals?' asked the king. 'If you watch them closely all day long and can tell me in the evening what they have eaten and what they have drunk, you may marry my daughter the princess. But if you cannot, I will see that you are given three lashes with the whip across your back. How's that for a bargain?'

The young fellow thought this an easy task which would present no difficulty at all.

Early next morning the head groom let the seven foals out of the stable. Off they sped, followed by the young fellow, over hill and dale, through woods and wide pastures. Before he had run many miles he was thoroughly tired of looking after the foals.

At length they came to a deep valley where an old woman sat spinning. When she saw the young fellow running after the foals with the sweat pouring down his brow, she called, 'Come here, my lad, and let me comb your hair!'

He did not need much persuading. He sank down exhausted beside the old woman and let her comb his hair. As the sun sank towards the horizon, he decided to go home. 'I had best go straight home,' he declared, 'for I can hardly go back to the palace now!'

'Wait until it is dark,' said the old woman, 'for then the foals will return and you can run along with them. There is no need for anyone to know that you have been lazing about here all day, instead of looking after them.'

When the foals came back the old woman gave the boy a little bottle of water and a tuft of moss, telling him to show them to the king and tell him that this was what the foals had eaten and drunk.

'Well?' asked the king, when the boy returned to the palace. 'Did you watch them carefully all day long?'

'Indeed, I did,' replied the youth.

'Can you tell me what they ate and drank?'

Then the young fellow produced the bottle of water and tuft of moss, saying, 'Here is what they ate and drank.'

The king knew immediately how well the boy had

looked after his foals, and he was so furious that he ordered his grooms to tie him up and give him three powerful lashes with the whip and then send him home. You can guess how he liked that!

Next morning the second son told his father that he wanted to go out into the world to seek his fortune. His parents tried their hardest to dissuade him, showing him the three ugly red weals on his brother's back, but he was so persistent that at last they had to give in and let him go.

After he had walked for a whole day, he came to the king's palace, as his brother had done. The king was standing on the steps, and called, 'Where are you going?' The young fellow replied that he was looking for a job, and immediately the king asked him if he would like to enter the royal service and look after seven foals. The king made the same conditions as for his elder brother, and the youth accepted them gladly, for he thought it would be no difficult task to tell what the foals ate and drank during the day.

Early next morning the chief groom opened the stable and let out the seven foals, which galloped away furiously over hill and dale with the boy running along behind them. But he fared no better than his elder brother. He was ready to drop with exhaustion when he came to the deep valley where the old woman sat spinning.

'Come here, my fine young fellow!' she cried. 'Come and let me comb your hair.' This suggestion sounded tempting to the lad, so he let the foals thunder away into the distance while he sat down and made himself comfortable.

When dusk fell the foals returned, and the old woman gave the boy a bottle of water and a tuft of moss to show to the king. But the king was furious when he heard the same story – how the foals had eaten moss and drunk water. He ordered his men to give the young fellow three powerful lashes with the whip and send him home.

When he reached the hut in the forest the boy related his sad experiences, adding that he would think twice before looking for a job another time.

On the third morning Cinders decided that he would go to seek his fortune too, for he liked the idea of looking after the little foals. But his two elder brothers laughed at him and made fun of him, for they thought him a simpleton.

'If we fared so badly,' they said, 'how do you hope to do any better? You have never done anything but rummage round in the ashes.'

'Let me at least try,' he insisted. 'I have set my mind on it.' So off he went, and no one could stop him.

All day long he kept walking, until at dusk he came to the palace where his brothers had been. The king was standing out on the steps, and asked him where he was going.

'I am looking for work to do,' he replied.

'Where do you come from?' asked the king, who was unwilling to take anyone else into his service without knowing more about them.

So the young fellow admitted that his two elder brothers had tried to look after the foals, adding that he hoped to do rather better than they had done.

'Oh no!' exclaimed the king angrily. 'I've had quite enough of your good-for-nothing family. Off you go!'

'I quite understand, Your Majesty,' replied Cinders, 'but since I am here now, will you not at least let me have a try?'

'Oh, well,' replied the king, 'if you are quite set on

having the whip across your shoulders I suppose you may try.'

At dawn the next morning the chief groom opened the stable door and let out the foals. They galloped over hill and dale, through fields and forests, with Cinders close behind them. When they had been running for a good while they came to the deep valley where the old woman sat with her spinning-wheel. She cried out, 'Stop, my fine young fellow. Come and let me comb your hair!'

'Leave me alone,' called Cinders, as he rushed past breathlessly, and he grabbed one of the foals by the mane. To his surprise the foal turned his head and said quietly, 'You had better ride on my back, for we have a long way to go yet!' Cinders wasted no time, but leapt nimbly astride the foal's back.

On and on they went, the miles stretching away behind them. 'Can you see anything?' asked the foal.

'No,' replied Cinders. 'I can see nothing.' So on they went for another few miles.

'Can you see anything yet?' asked the foal.

'No,' replied Cinders, 'I still cannot see anything.'

On they went for many more miles before the foal again asked, 'Can you see anything now?'

'Oh yes. I see something white gleaming in the distance, rather like an enormous birch tree.'

'That's where we are making for,' said the foal.

When they reached the birch tree the eldest foal uprooted it with his teeth, revealing a door in the ground. It opened into a little underground chamber, bare of furniture except for a fireplace and a few branches. Behind the door, however, lay an old, rusty sword, a bottle and a jug.

'Can you wield this sword?' asked the foal. But Cinders could not even raise it from the ground. Then he

13

was told to drink out of the bottle, and suddenly he found that he could brandish the sword through the air with the greatest of ease, for it felt as light as a feather.

'Take the sword with you,' said the foal. 'On the day when you marry the princess you must cut off all our heads with it. For we are all princes, brothers of the princess who will be your bride if you can tell the king what we have eaten and what we have drunk. When you have cut off our heads, you must lay each head on top of the tail to which it belongs, for a wicked troll bewitched us many long years ago, and only in this way can he be deprived of his power over us.'

Cinders promised to do as he was instructed, and they continued on their way. After they had covered many more miles, the foal asked, 'Can you see anything?' But Cinders saw nothing. Many more miles rolled away behind them, and again the foal asked, 'Can you see anything yet?'

'Yes, I can. Far away in the distance I see a sort of blue ribbon.'

'That is the river,' replied the foal. 'We must cross over to the far side.'

A beautiful arched bridge led over the river, and

again they galloped on for many miles. Once again the foal asked, 'Can you see anything?'

'Yes, in the far distance I see a black spire, rather like a chapel.'

'That's where we are going.'

When the foals cantered into the courtyard they suddenly turned into princes wearing magnificent clothes that gleamed and flashed with gold and silver. Into the church they went and received bread and wine from the priest at the altar. Cinders followed them, and when the priest had blessed them they filed out of the church again. But Cinders took with him some bread and a tiny bottle of wine from the altar.

Before the princes left the churchyard they had once again become foals, and they returned the same way as they had come – only faster than ever. Swift as the wind they sped over the bridge, past the silver birch tree, past the old woman and her spinning-wheel. They were going so fast, that they could not hear what the old woman shouted after them. Darkness was falling when they reached the palace.

The king was waiting for Cinders on the palace steps. 'Well?' he asked. 'Have you kept a good eye on my foals all day long?'

'I have done my best,' replied Cinders.

'Then you will be able to tell me what they ate and drank?'

Cinders took the bread and wine from his pocket and showed them to the king, saying, 'You see here, Your Majesty, what they have eaten and drunk.'

'Now I know that you are telling the truth and that you have looked after them well and loyally,' declared the king. 'Your reward is the princess for your bride, and half my kingdom.'

The wedding was celebrated with great pomp. As they sat down to the wedding feast, Cinders excused himself, saying that he wanted to fetch something. Down to the stable he ran, and he cut off all the foals' heads with the old rusty sword, beginning with the eldest and finishing with the youngest. Carefully he laid each head on the tail of the body to which it belonged, and suddenly the seven princes stood before him, wreathed in smiles. The king's joy knew no bounds when they all strode into the wedding banquet, and the princess loved Cinders more than ever.

'One half of my kingdom is yours now,' said the king, 'and the other half will be yours after my death. Now that my sons are princes again, they are quite capable of finding new kingdoms for themselves.'

Never had there been such a superb feast. I was there too, but no one had time to think of me. I was given only bread and butter, and I laid it on the stove. The bread burned and the butter melted away, so I had nothing at the feast after all!

Golden-hairs and Golden-stars

There was once a king who was determined to marry none but the most beautiful and most virtuous girl in the land. At last he found a golden-haired bride who was so beautiful that one could never weary of gazing at her. The king loved her with all his heart, and took her for his wife.

But the king's mother also lived in the palace. She was deeply jealous of the young queen and was always looking for some way to harm her.

About a year after the wedding the young queen gave birth to a baby boy. He was a beautiful child, and he had three little golden hairs behind his ear. Before anyone could see the new-born child, the old queen took him and wrapped him in a shawl, as if she were going to lay him in the cradle. In reality, however, she put him in a wooden box. She closed the lid, carried the box down to the river and dropped it into the water to float away down-stream. Then the wicked old woman wrapped a tom-cat in another shawl, and laid it in the cradle.

Early next morning the king came with his courtiers to see the heir to the throne, and they were all horrified at the baby's hairy black face. It was a cat. The poor queen wept and could not utter a word. The king's wicked old mother remained silent. But she told the king afterwards that – lovely though his wife was – it was clear that she must be a witch, since she had given birth to a cat.

A year went by, and the young queen gave birth to a little daughter, the loveliest child the sun had ever shone on, with three little golden stars behind her ear. Once again the wicked old woman took the child and sent it down the river. Then she wrapped a tabby-cat in a shawl and laid it in the cradle. This time the king was almost angry with his wife, but still he loved her dearly and refused to believe what his mother told him about her. The young queen wept day and night, and bore no more children, and everyone thought now that she really was a witch.

But on the night the king's son was born, a fisherman had cast his net into the river. All at once he heard a baby crying in the darkness. He rowed towards the sound, saw the floating wooden box, fished it out of the water and found the baby boy inside. Full of happiness,

he hurried home to his wife and said, 'Guess what I have brought you in this box!'

Her guesses came nowhere near the truth, so he lifted the lid and showed her the baby, who by this time was fast asleep. 'We have no children of our own,' he said, 'so God must have sent us this gift.' The woman laughed with joy and happiness. She unwrapped the shawl and found rich garments and linen beneath it, together with a little money. She looked at him carefully and discovered the three tiny gold hairs behind his ear, and so they called him Golden-hairs.

They brought the child up as their own son, but they kept the money and the baby clothes safe in the box, for they had enough money of their own even with an extra mouth to feed. 'Who knows?' they said. 'Perhaps he will need the money some day.'

A year passed by, and once again the man fished a wooden box from the water, and found in it a beautiful baby girl. He brought her home and as she was wrapped in a shawl as rich as the little boy's, with the same amount of money hidden in it, the fisher-folk believed that the children must be brother and sister. They kept the child as their own daughter, and called her Golden-stars, because of the three little stars they found behind her ear.

Golden-hairs and Golden-stars grew up together in the house of the fisherman and his wife, who cared for them as if they had been their own children. One day when they had been playing with their friends, they came rushing breathlessly into the house and asked, 'Father, Mother, is it true that we are not your real children, that we are orphans, and Father fished us out of the river?'

What could the couple do but tell the truth? They fetched the wooden boxes and showed the children the things which had been kept safe for them all these years.

When the children had seen everything, they said, 'Thank you, dear Mother and Father, for your kind care and protection all these years. But now we must go out into the world and find our real parents.'

So they packed their bags and set out. For many days they wandered, asking here and there, but no one could tell them anything. They came to a great city, and as they were tired of travelling they found a house and settled there. Soon they had made the house and garden so beautiful that the whole city was talking of Golden-hairs and Golden-stars.

In the very same city was the castle of the king and queen, but the children had no idea that they were so near their parents. The news of Golden-hairs and Golden-stars had reached even as far as the king's court. The king's old mother knew immediately from the names whose children they were, for she had seen the golden hairs and the golden stars behind their ears.

Day and night she racked her brain for a scheme to do away with the children. At length she hatched an evil plot. Disguised as a poor old woman, she went to the children's house. With false, sweet-sounding words, she praised the house and garden. 'What a lovely house you have!' she exclaimed. 'And you, my sweet ones, are both so young and beautiful. May I see the garden too, my daughter? I have heard so many wonderful things about it.' In the garden her flattery knew no bounds. 'What a superb garden! Did you really grow all these exquisite flowers yourselves, my lambkin? And you, my cherub, you must have planted all these trees so beautifully. But how perfect it would be if only you had a little bell on each tree! How wonderful it would sound!'

'Where can we find such bells?' asked Golden-hairs at once.

'Do you see that hill over there? At the very top you will find a great garden filled with trees, and on each tree hangs a little golden bell. You have only to take one and hang it in your garden, and overnight a little bell will grow on each tree. Oh yes, if only you had a little bell like that.'

So saying, she departed, like a lean year that leaves its mark behind it. She was sending the children straight into the jaws of death, for the garden on the hill was enchanted. Whoever stayed there for longer than an hour turned into a tree and never left the garden again.

When the old woman had gone, the children wondered what they should do.

'I will go and fetch a golden bell,' said Golden-hairs.

'No, brother. Do not go,' pleaded Golden-stars. 'Who knows what will happen to you there!' But her brother was not to be dissuaded.

'Then at least do not spend long there, and come back as quickly as you can,' said Golden-stars.

Early next morning he climbed the hill and came into the garden, which stretched away and away without end. He reached up on tiptoe, tore down one of the little bells, and without looking back, raced down the hill as if pursued by evil spirits. When he reached home he hung the bell on a tree, and the next morning the whole garden rang with the loveliest chimes.

Once again the old woman came and spoke with honeyed words. 'My dearest little daughter, what beautiful chimes you have in your garden now! But you should have little golden fishes in your fountain; then you would have a garden more beautiful than any other.'

'Where can we find such fishes?'

'Up on the hill you will find a pool, my boy,' she said, and slipped quietly away.

Early next morning Golden-hairs climbed the hill to fetch the little fishes. He found the pool, caught a fish and ran home with it as fast as he could. Next morning the fountain was alive with glittering, golden fishes, darting hither and thither, a joy to behold.

The old woman heard of it and wondered how the boy had escaped from the enchanted garden. She thought out a new plan which was sure to bring the children to grief – if not both of them, then at least one.

For a third time she came to their house and admired their beautiful garden, saying, 'Lovely, really lovely, my little doves! But there is still one thing missing, and that is the bird of truth.'

'Where can I find this bird?'

'Up on the hill, my dear heart. At the furthest end of the garden stands a beautiful big house, and in a room at the far end of the house you will find the bird of truth, sitting on the stove.' And she went on her way, laughing cruelly to herself, for now one of the children must surely be doomed.

'I must have the bird of truth,' declared Golden-hairs, when the old woman had waddled away, 'even if it costs me my life.'

Golden-stars did her very best to hold him back. She wept and pleaded with him, but all to no avail. When they awoke at dawn she made one more attempt. 'Please do not go, brother. I have such fear in my heart. I dreamt about you all night, terrible dreams. Don't go, brother, or you will die.'

But Golden-hairs would not be persuaded, and off he went up the mountain. This time he did not hurry as he had done before, but dawdled through the garden, looking at all the trees and flowers. When he reached the furthest end of the garden he saw the big house and slipped inside. The first room glistened with pure silver, the second room was of gold, the third sparkled with precious stones, the fourth was studded with gleaming jewels, and everywhere he went he gazed in wonder. At last he came to the room at the furthest end of the house, and saw the bird of truth perched on the stove. As he stretched out his hand to take it, the hour was up, and – tinkle, tinkle – he fell to the gound, a tiny piece of glass.

For a whole day and night Golden-stars waited for her brother, but he did not come. The following morning

she dressed and climbed the hill to look for him, tears flowing down her cheeks. As she wandered round the edge of the garden, not knowing what to do, she met an old woman, who took pity on her and gave her some useful advice. Golden-stars listened carefully, and then she ran through the enchanted garden, through the silver and golden rooms, without once looking to right or left, gathered into her apron all the pieces of glass she found lying on the ground, seized the bird of truth and then made straight for home again. But the moment she left the enchanted garden – plop! plop! plop! – the pieces of glass fell from her apron and turned into all the children who had ever tried to catch the bird of truth. Amongst them was her dear lost brother. She took him by the hand at once and hurried back home with him. And as soon as they reached their house they put the bird of truth in a cage.

Before long the entire city had heard about the little golden bells, the golden fishes in the fountain and the bird of truth, and at last the king and queen also heard about them and came to see these wonderful things. They were delighted with the bells and the fishes and were amazed to hear that nothing was hidden from the bird of truth. At once they began to ask the bird what had become of their own two children, and whether they were still alive. The bird began to speak and related everything that had happened to Golden-hairs and Golden-stars since they had been sent floating down the river as tiny babies. How overjoyed the king and queen were to find their long-lost children! The parents had found their children, and the children had found their parents. But then the bird went on to tell them that the king's mother was to blame for everything. Angrily the king ordered her to be shut in a wooden box and floated down the river, as the children had been so many years ago. Who knows where the river has carried her!

At the palace there was a great feast to celebrate the children's home-coming. Hundreds of guests were invited, but they forgot to ask you and me. And as we were not there, we saw nothing and can tell nothing more.

The Water of Life

There was once a king who was so ill that nobody thought he would survive. His three sons were very sad and went down to weep in the palace garden. There they met an old man who asked them what was their sorrow. They told him that their father was so ill he was sure to die, for there was nothing that could help him.

'I know one more remedy,' said the old man. 'The

water of life. If he drinks of that, he will be cured. But it is hard to find.'

'I will find it,' declared the eldest son, and went to ask the king's permission to go in search of the water of life, for it was the only possible cure.

'No,' replied the king. 'The danger is too great. I would rather die.' But the boy went on pleading until the king gave in. The boy secretly thought that if he brought the water his father would love him above the others and would leave him the whole kingdom.

He set out, and before he had ridden far a dwarf suddenly stood before him on the path and called out to him, 'Whither away so fast?'

'Stupid manikin! It is none of your business,' said the prince disdainfully, and rode on.

The little man was angered by this, and made a bad wish. Soon afterwards the prince came to a narrow ravine, and the further he rode the closer together drew the rocky walls, until the path became so narrow that he could not go a single step further. He could neither turn his horse nor dismount, so there he sat, held tight as a prisoner.

For a long time the sick king waited for his son, but he did not return. So the second son said, 'Let me go, Father, to look for the water of life.' But he thought to himself that if his brother were dead he would inherit the kingdom.

At first the king tried to hold him back, but at length he gave in. The prince took the same route as his brother had taken and met the dwarf, who stopped him and asked him where he was going in such a hurry.

'Foolish little manikin! It is none of your business,' said the prince. And he rode on without looking back. But the dwarf set a spell on him, and the prince rode into

a deep ravine, as his brother had done. There he stuck fast, unable to move either forward or back.

When the second son failed to return, the youngest son begged the king to be allowed to try his luck, and at last the king let him go. Before long he met the dwarf, who asked him, 'Whither away so fast?'

The young prince drew rein and stopped to answer him. 'I am looking for the water of life, for my father is desperately ill.'

'Do you know where to look for it?'

'No,' replied the prince.

'As you have behaved courteously towards me, unlike your two arrogant brothers, I will tell you where to find it. It bubbles up out of a well in the courtyard of an enchanted castle. But you will not be able to enter the

courtyard unless I give you an iron rod and two small loaves of bread. With the rod you must strike the great iron gate of the courtyard three times, and it will swing open for you. Inside in the courtyard lie two lions, with wide-open jaws. Throw them each a loaf of bread, and they will trouble you no further. Hurry then and fetch the water from the well before midday, for if you are late the gate will clang to behind you and you will be unable to escape.'

The prince thanked the dwarf, took the rod and the loaves and continued on his way. When he reached the castle he found everything exactly as the dwarf had said. The gate sprang open at the third rap of the iron rod, and as soon as he had calmed the lions with the two loaves, he entered the castle and found himself in a large and beautiful hall. There sat enchanted princes, and beside them on the bench lay a sword and a loaf. These he took with him.

Next he came to a room where he found a beautiful maiden. She seemed overjoyed to see him, kissed him and said, 'You have freed me from enchantment. Your reward shall be my kingdom, and we shall be married when you return in a year's time.' Then she told him how to reach the well of the water of life, but warned him to hurry and draw the water before it struck midday.

The prince went on and came at length to a room in which stood a beautiful bed. He was very tired and lay down to rest, and soon he fell asleep. As he awoke he heard the clock from the great tower striking a quarter to twelve. He leapt to his feet in a fright, ran to the well and filled a basin which he found lying beside it, and then made haste to get out of the castle. Twelve o'clock was striking just as he ran through the great iron gate, which clanged shut so violently that part of his heel was left behind.

But he was happy to have found the water of life and hastened homeward. On the way he met the dwarf again and thanked him for his help.

'You have two great treasures there!' said the dwarf, when he saw the sword and the little loaf. 'With the sword you will be able to overcome whole armies, and the loaf will always remain whole.'

The prince did not want to return home without his two brothers. 'Dear dwarf,' he said, 'can you tell me where my two brothers are? They set out to look for the water of life before me but failed to return home.'

'They are shut in between two mountains,' replied the dwarf, 'making amends for their arrogance.' The prince begged so persistently for their release that at length the dwarf gave in, but he warned him, 'Beware of them, for they have wicked hearts!'

As soon as his brothers appeared, the young prince told them how glad he was to see them, and related how he had found the water of life and brought back a basinful of it. 'I also freed a beautiful princess from enchantment,' he said. 'We are to be married next year and I shall be given a great kingdom.'

They rode on together and came to a land where there was famine and war. The king of that country was so desperate that he was on the point of surrendering. The young prince took him his little loaf, instructing him to feed his whole kingdom with it; he also gave the king his sword, with which he soon overcame all his enemies, and his land settled down into peaceful ways once again.

The prince took back his loaf and sword, and the three brothers rode on. As time went on they passed through two other kingdoms which were being ruined by war and famine, and each time the prince gave the kings his loaf and his sword, and soon he had saved three kingdoms.

The brothers came to the coast and set sail in a ship. On the voyage the two elder brothers murmured together, saying, 'Our young brother found the water of life and not we, and our father is sure to reward him by giving him the kingdom, which is ours by rights. He will take away our fortune.' They swore to be avenged and plotted together to ruin their brother. They waited till he was asleep, and then they poured the water of life into their own bottles, replacing it with sea-water.

When they reached home the youngest son took his father the basin of water, but no sooner had the king drunk a little of it than he became worse than before. As he groaned and lamented, the two elder sons came and accused their young brother of trying to poison him. They said that they would give the king the water of life, and offered it to him. No sooner had the king taken a sip of it than he felt his illness fade, and soon he was as healthy and strong as he had ever been.

The two elder sons went and jeered at their younger brother, and told him what they had done while he was asleep on board ship. 'You did all the work and took all the risk,' they said, 'but we have all the thanks and the reward! You should have kept your wits about you. When the year is up, one of us will claim your beautiful princess. Do not dare betray us. Father would not believe you, in any case. If we hear you have said a single word, you'll pay with your life. If you keep quiet, nothing will happen to you.'

The old king was angry with his youngest son, for he believed that he had tried to murder him. He called his court together and pronounced sentence on the boy. He was to be shot in secret.

One day the young prince rode out hunting in the company of the king's chief huntsman, suspecting nothing. When they were alone in the heart of the forest the prince saw the huntsman looking at him with great sadness, and asked, 'What is troubling you, dear huntsman?'

'I cannot tell you – and yet I should,' replied the huntsman.

'Tell me what is the matter,' said the prince. 'Whatever it is, I will not hold it against you.'

'Alas,' said the huntsman. 'The king has ordered me to shoot you!'

The prince was terrified, and said, 'Please let me live,

dear huntsman. I will give you my royal robes in exchange for your livery.'

'Willingly,' replied the huntsman. 'I could not have brought myself to shoot you.' So they changed clothes and the huntsman returned home. But the prince went further into the forest.

After a time, three waggon-loads of gold and precious stones arrived at the court for the young prince, sent by the three kings whose kingdoms he had saved from war and famine. This made the old king wonder. Could his youngest son have been innocent after all? 'If only he were still alive!' he said to the courtiers who stood round about. 'How sorry I am that I ordered his death!'

'He is still alive,' declared the huntsman. 'I could not bring myself to carry out your order.' He told the king exactly what had happened, and a great weight fell from the king's heart. He issued a proclamation in every land, begging his son to return home, for he was forgiven.

The princess whom the youngest son had released from enchantment ordered a path to be made up to her castle, gold and glistening. She told her servants that the prince who rode straight up over the gold would be the right one and that they should admit him. But anyone who rode up beside the golden path would be the wrong prince and should be turned away.

When the year was almost up, the eldest brother thought he would go to claim the princess, together with her kingdom. Off he rode, but when he came to the path of gold he thought it would be a shame to ride on it; so he turned off to the right and rode on the grass beside the path. When he reached the castle gate the guards told him that he was not the right prince and could not be admitted, and they turned him away.

Soon after this the second brother set out to claim the princess. His horse placed one hoof on the golden path, but the prince was afraid of scratching the gold, so he turned off to the left and rode on the grass beside the path till he came to the castle gate. But the guards told him he was not the right prince and turned him away.

A whole year had now gone by, and the youngest brother decided to leave the forest and ride to his beloved, and so forget his sorrows. He set out, thinking of nothing but the princess and how he longed to be with her. And so he did not see the path of gold. His horse galloped straight up the middle of the path to the castle gate, which swung open. The princess welcomed the prince with joy, saying that he had set her free and should be lord of the kingdom. And their marriage was celebrated with great happiness and joy.

After the wedding his bride told the prince that the king had forgiven him, so he rode to tell his father how his two elder brothers had deceived him, forcing him to keep silence. The old king wanted to punish them for their wickedness, but they had taken ship and fled across the seas, never to return.

King Thrushbeard

A king had an extremely beautiful daughter, but she was so proud and arrogant that no suitor was good enough for her. One after another they were laughed out of the palace in scorn. At last the king held a great banquet to which he invited anyone who wanted to marry the princess. All the suitors were drawn up in a line, in order of rank and social position; first came the kings, then the princes, dukes, counts, barons, and finally the noblemen.

The princess was led along the ranks, but she made some objection to each of her suitors. One was too fat, 'a beer barrel', she called him. Another was too thin, 'like a scarecrow', she said. A third was too short, 'a miserable dwarf'; a fourth was 'pale as a ghost'; a fifth was too red, 'just like a cock's comb!'; a sixth was too old, 'a green log dried at the fire'. She had some sharp words for every one of her suitors. The one who amused her most of all, however, was a good king whose chin was a little crooked. 'Do look at that!' she laughed. 'He has a chin like a thrush's beak!' After that he was known as 'Thrushbeard'.

The old king was very angry when he saw that she just made fun of all her suitors, and swore that she should marry the very first beggar to present himself at the palace door.

A few days later a wandering minstrel came to sing beneath the palace window, hoping to earn a few coppers. 'Bid him come up,' said the king, when he heard of it. So the minstrel came upstairs in his dirty, ragged old clothes, and played and sang for the king and his daughter. When he had finished he held out his hand for their charity. 'Your singing has pleased me so well,' declared the king, 'that I offer you my daughter to be your wife.'

The princess was dismayed, but the king told her that he had sworn she should marry the first beggar to present himself. He would not listen to her pleadings, but sent for the priest, who married them on the spot. After the ceremony was over the king declared, 'It is unseemly

that a beggar's wife should remain in my palace, so off you go with your husband.'

The beggar took her by the hand and led her away, and she had no choice but to go with him, on foot. When they came to a deep forest she asked, 'Who owns this beautiful forest?'

'It belongs to King Thrushbeard. It would have belonged to you too if you had married him.'

'How wayward and foolish I have been. I wish I had married King Thrushbeard!' she sighed.

Not long after, they crossed a wide meadow. 'Who owns this lovely green meadow?' she asked.

'It belongs to King Thrushbeard. It would have belonged to you too if you had married him.'

'How wayward and foolish I have been. If only I had married King Thrushbeard!' she sighed.

Soon they passed through a noble city. 'Who owns this fine big city?' she asked.

'It belongs to King Thrushbeard,' replied the beggar. 'If you had married him it would have belonged to you too.'

'How wayward and foolish I have been. How I wish I had married King Thrushbeard!'

'I do not like to hear you always wishing your husband were another man,' said the beggar. 'What is wrong with me? Am I not good enough for you?'

At last they came to a tiny hut, and she said, 'What is this miserable shack? Who owns this wretched hovel?'

'This is your house and my house, my dear,' replied the beggar. 'Take care not to bump your head in the doorway!'

'But where are all the servants?' asked the princess in despair.

'Servants?' answered the man. 'You must do everything for yourself here. Come on now, light the fire and prepare my supper quickly, for I am tired and hungry.'

But the princess had no notion how to lay a fire or cook, and the beggar had to help her. As soon as they had finished their meagre meal they lay down to sleep. Next morning he made her get up at the crack of dawn to do the housework. For a few days they muddled through in this way until all their food was used up. At last the man said, 'It can't go on like this, wife. We are eating and yet doing nothing to earn our food. You will have to weave baskets.' So out he went and gathered willows, which he brought home to her, and she tried to weave them into baskets, but soon her hands were cut and sore from the hard willows.

'This is not going to do us much good!' said the man. 'Perhaps you can spin better?' So she sat down and tried to spin, but the coarse thread cut into her soft fingers until they bled.

'This is not getting us very far either,' said the man. 'I have made a very poor marriage! What can you do? Let us try to start a pottery business – I will make the pots and plates and mugs, and you can sit in the market place and sell them.'

'Oh dear,' she thought, 'if people from my father's kingdom pass by and see me selling pottery, how they will laugh at me!' But she had to do it if she was not to starve to death.

To begin with all went well, for the people were attracted by her pretty face and willingly paid what she asked for her wares. Many people even gave her money and left their pots with her. But one day as she sat surrounded by her pots and plates and mugs at the corner of the market, a drunken hussar came careering along on his horse and rode straight through her wares, shattering them into a thousand fragments. She burst into tears, terrified of what her husband would say. 'What can I do?' she cried. 'What will my husband say?' Home she ran and told him tearfully what had happened.

'Whatever made you sit at the *corner* of the market place with pottery?' he exclaimed scornfully. 'Stop crying, woman. I see now that you are not fit for any kind of work. But I have been to the royal palace, and the king's chamberlain has promised you a place as a scullery maid. There at least you will be given your food.'

So the princess became a scullery maid and had to run after the cook and do all the dirtiest, greasiest and most unpleasant work. At night she went home with a little dish of left-overs in each pocket, and this had to do for their supper and breakfast.

The day came when the prince's wedding was to be

celebrated in the palace, and the poor girl went and stood at the entrance to the great hall to watch. As the lights went up and the guests in their magnificent robes began to arrive, she cursed her pride and arrogance, comparing her own wretched fate and her poverty with the wealth and splendour which she saw displayed around her. From time to time the footmen would fling her a few left-overs and crumbs of the exquisite food they were carrying in and out, and these she stuffed into two little pots in her pockets to take home with her.

All at once the king's son himself approached her, dressed in velvet and silk, with gold chains about his neck. When he saw the beautiful young woman standing by the door, he took her by the hand to dance with her. She drew back in alarm, for she saw that he was the King Thrushbeard who had wanted to marry her and whom she had driven away with taunts and sneers. But her struggles were of no avail, and he drew her into the ballroom. The little pots fell from her pockets, so that the soup and left-overs fell all over the floor. What a shout of mocking laughter arose when the people saw it! The princess was so ashamed that she wished the earth would open and swallow her up. She turned and fled, but a man caught her on the stairs and brought her back. When she looked at him she saw that it was again King Thrushbeard.

'Do not be afraid,' he said gently. 'I and the beggar minstrel who married you are one and the same person. I was also the drunken hussar who broke up all your pots and plates with his horse. I disguised myself to rid you of your pride and arrogance, but I did it for love of you.'

She wept bitterly and said, 'I have done you great wrong, and I am unworthy to be your wife.'

'Be comforted,' he said. 'The days of sadness are over,

and now we must celebrate our marriage.' Then ladies-in-waiting dressed her in magnificent robes, and her father was sent for. The entire court wished her great happiness in her union with King Thrushbeard, and so the true rejoicing began. I wish that you and I had been there too.

Robin Redbreast

In olden times there lived in the parish of Guirek in Brittany a poor widow called Ninorch Madek. She was the daughter of a rich nobleman, who, on his death, had left a castle and estate, a mill and a tile-kiln, as well as twelve horses and twice as many oxen, twelve cows and ten times as many sheep, not to mention the crops and the household linen.

But the poor widow's brothers, who should have protected their sister's interests, withheld her share of the inheritance. The eldest brother, Perrik, took the castle, the estate and the horses. Fanche, the second brother, took the mill and the cows. Riwal, the youngest brother was given the oxen, the sheep and the tile-kiln. Nothing was left for poor Ninorch but a tumbledown hut without a door, out on the heathland, which once had been used as a shelter for sick cattle.

While the poor widow was moving her few household possessions into this miserable hovel, her brother Fanche seemed to take pity on her, for he said, 'I should like to deal kindly with you, so I am giving you this black cow. It is very thin and not very strong, and will hardly give enough milk to nourish a new-born child, so it is not much use to me. Keep it, and Mayflower can take it out to pasture every day.'

Mayflower was Ninorch's daughter, a child of eleven, as pale and as delicate as the white hawthorn blossom, and so it was that everyone called her Mayflower.

The widow took the cow, and sent Mayflower with it every day to the pasture. Mayflower would spend the whole day on the heath, tending the cow while it nibbled the few blades of grass that managed to grow on the stony soil. She would weave garlands of wild broom, praying aloud as she wove.

One day as she was singing a hymn which she had heard in the church at Guirek, she noticed a little robin perching on one of the garlands she had woven. It began to chirp, cocked its head on one side and looked at Mayflower as if it were trying to tell her something. She stepped a little closer to it, trying to make out what it was saying, but could not understand a word. The robin became almost frantic, fluttering its wings and hopping up and down at her feet, but she could make nothing of its twitterings. The tiny bird's antics so absorbed her that she did not notice the dusk falling. Stars were already twinkling in the sky when the robin took to the air and flew off into the night.

Quickly Mayflower ran to see what had happened to her cow, but she could not find it anywhere on the wide heath. She called at the top of her voice, rattled with her stick in all the bushes, climbed up to the little pools where the rain water collected, but all in vain. At last she heard her mother's voice in the distance, calling for her as if something dreadful had happened. She hurried to her mother, and found her not far from the hut, standing beside the cow's body, which had been torn and half devoured by wolves.

Mayflower was filled with sorrow at the sight. She fell on her knees and wept bitterly. Her mother tried to comfort her, saying, 'All creatures have to die some day, my dear. We are all at the mercy of wolves and wicked men, but God will protect us. Come, help me to gather my twigs and let us go home. What is done cannot be undone.'

Mayflower did as her mother bade her, but at each step she sighed deeply, and tears raced one another down her cheeks. She was so miserable that she could not eat a bite of supper, and she lay awake all night long, thinking she could hear the cow mooing at the door.

Next morning she rose early and hurried up on to the heath, barefoot and wearing only a thin cotton dress. On the same broom garland she saw the same little robin that had given her so much pleasure on the previous day. Once again it seemed to be trying to speak to her, but still she could make no sense of its twitterings. Angrily she turned to go, but suddenly she spied in the grass what seemed to be a gold coin. She placed her bare foot on it to feel it, but it was only a golden flower ... a golden flower, which could grant all those who trod on it barefoot the power to understand and to speak the language of the beasts of the field and the birds of the air.

Scarcely had she set her foot upon the flower than she began to understand exactly what the robin was saying to her. 'Mayflower,' it said, 'I have come to help you. Will you listen to me?'

'Who are you, then?' asked Mayflower, still astonished at finding herself suddenly able to understand the bird.

'I am Robin Redbreast,' answered the bird. 'I followed Christ to the Cross on Calvary, and with my beak I broke off a thorn which was scratching His brow. As a reward for this service God the Father lengthened my life until the day of judgement and gave me power to make one poor girl rich every year. For this year I have chosen you.'

'Is that true, Robin Redbreast?' said Mayflower joyfully. 'Then shall I be able to wear a silver cross round my neck, and shall I have enough money to buy myself a pair of wooden shoes?'

'You shall have a golden cross round your neck,' replied the robin, 'and wear a pair of silken shoes, as the noblewomen do.'

'What must I do, then, dear bird, to earn this good fortune?'

'You have only to follow wherever I lead you.'

Mayflower followed wherever the robin led her, and so crossed the wide heath and came at last to the sand-dunes which faced the seven islands. There the bird stopped, turned to her and said, 'Do you not see something in the sand at your feet?'

'Indeed, I do,' said Mayflower. 'I see a pair of big wooden shoes and a staff of holly wood, untouched by any knife.'

'Put on the shoes and take up the holly staff,' ordered the robin. 'Now you must walk across the sea until you come to the first island. There you will find a great rock and a clump of sea-green rushes. Weave a rope with the rushes and strike the rock with your stick. A cow will come out. Throw your rope round her neck and lead her home to your mother.'

Mayflower did as the robin had said. She crossed the sea, wove the rope of rushes and struck the rock with her stick, and immediately a beautiful white cow appeared before her. Its eyes were as gentle as a spaniel's, its coat as shiny as a mole's, and its udder was soft with silky white down. How happy Mayflower was, and how happy her mother would be!

The robin had told her that the cow's name was Mor-Vyoch, which means sea-cow, because she had come out of the sea. When Ninorch tried to milk Mor-Vyoch the milk ran on and on through her fingers, as if it would never stop. Ninorch filled all her earthenware pots and dishes, then her wooden butter-churn and her tubs, and still the milk flowed.

'Dear Mother of God!' she exclaimed. 'When has a cow ever given so much milk?'

The sea-cow's milk seemed never-ending. She gave enough milk to feed all the children in the entire land. Soon everyone for miles around could talk of nothing but Ninorch's cow, and people came from far and near to see the wonderful animal. Even the priest came, for he wanted to be quite certain that the devil had no hand in the strange affair. But he had to admit that no mortal soul had anything to fear from the beast.

All the richest farmers round about wanted to buy Ninorch's cow, and each tried to outbid the other. Perrik, her eldest brother, came too, and said, 'If you are a good Christian, sister, you will not forget that I am your brother, and will give me preference over all the others. Sell me Mor-Vyoch and I will give you nine cows in exchange.'

'Mor-Vyoch is worth far more than nine cows,' Ninorch replied. 'She is worth all the cows in this whole land! I can supply all the markets with milk, butter and cheese.'

'Very well, sister,' said Perrik. 'Give me the cow and I will give you the whole of our father's estate where you were born, the estate, with the cattle and everything else that goes with it.'

42

Ninorch accepted this offer, but not before she had been taken to the family estate and, following the ancient custom of Brittany, had dug a clod of earth, drunk water from the well, lit a fire on the hearth and cut a few hairs from the tail of every horse in the stables, to prove that she owned all these things. Then she handed Mor-Vyoch over to her brother Perrik, who led the animal far away to a house which he possessed on the coast.

When Mayflower saw Mor-Vyoch being led away she burst into tears. Nothing would console her. At nightfall she went to the stables to see that there was plenty of hay in the mangers and water in the drinking-troughs, and as she worked she sighed, 'Why did they have to take the Mor-Vyoch away? When shall I ever see her again?'

Scarcely had the words left her lips than she heard a gentle mooing behind her, and as she understood the language of all animals she knew at once that it meant, 'Here I am!'

Quick as a flash she turned and saw the sea-cow standing there as large as life. 'Is it really you?' she exclaimed. 'Who brought you back?'

'I could not live with your Uncle Perrik. He is too heavily laden with sins. I belong to you, as before.'

'But does that mean my mother will have to give back the estate and all the horses?'

'Not at all!' replied Mor-Vyoch. 'The estate belongs to you, for your uncle deprived you and your mother of your rights in the first place.'

'But my uncle will return here to claim you.'

'Yes, indeed, so you must run quickly into the garden and pluck three sprigs of vervain. When you bring them to me, I will tell you what to do with them.'

Not a moment did Mayflower waste, and in a few moments she returned with the sprigs of vervain.

'Now,' said the sea-cow, 'you must rub me all over with the herb, from the tip of my tail to my horns, and repeat three times: "Saint Ronan of Hybernia".'

Mayflower did as she was told, and on the third repetition the sea-cow suddenly turned into a magnificent chestnut horse! Mayflower's eyes almost popped out of her head.

'Will your Uncle Perrik be able to recognize me now?' asked the animal. 'Mor-Vyoch is no more. Now I am March-Mor.'

Next morning Ninorch wanted to try out the wonderful horse and send it to the market with some corn. What was her surprise to see that the more she loaded on to the animal's back, the longer its back became, so that it was able to carry a heavier load than all the other horses in the parish put together.

News of the wonderful horse soon spread far and wide, and before long it reached the ears of Fanche, the second brother. He came to inspect the horse, and offered to buy it from his sister, but she would not listen to him until he offered to give her in exchange the mill, with all the cows and everything else that went with it. Then she agreed to the exchange.

The bargain was concluded, and Ninorch took possession of the mill and Fanche took the sea-horse. But it was not yet evening when the horse returned to Mayflower and told her once again to rub it from the tip of its tail to the tips of its ears with vervain and to repeat "Saint Ronan of Hybernia" three times. In the twinkling of an eye, the horse changed into a beautiful sheep, heavily laden with rich scarlet wool, so long that it trailed on the ground, soft and shiny as spun flax. March-Mor was now Mor-Vauw, the sea-sheep.

Ninorch was astonished to see this new change, and called to Mayflower to fetch the shears. 'Look!' she said. 'The poor animal can hardly stand under the weight of its wool!'

She began to shear the fleece, but she had hardly begun when she discovered that the wool was growing almost as fast as she cut it. Her third brother, Riwal, passed that way as she was shearing, and he hastened to offer his tile-kiln and all his sheep as well as all the pasture-land in exchange for the wonderful animal. After a brief hesitation, his sister agreed.

But as Riwal was leading the sea-sheep along the coast it suddenly plunged into the waves and swam out to the smallest of the seven islands. The rock opened to admit the sheep, and Mor-Vauw returned no more to the land of men.

Next morning Mayflower ran out to the heath to find Robin Redbreast. 'I was waiting for you my child,' he said. 'Mor-Vauw has gone, and will not return. Your mother's three brothers are well punished for their greed. You are now rich enough to wear a golden cross and silk shoes, as I promised you. My task is accomplished and I must fly far, far away. But never forget, my child, that you were once poor, and that a small bird made you rich, with the help of God.'

In token of her gratitude Mayflower built a chapel out on the heath, over the place where she had first met Robin Redbreast. And old men who heard this story from their fathers can remember worshipping in the chapel when they were children.

East of the Sun and West of the Moon

There was once a woodcutter who had a great many children, but he was so poor that he was barely able to feed and clothe them. The children were all fine-looking boys and girls, but the most lovely by far was the youngest daughter.

One Thursday night in late autumn, a fierce storm was raging outside. It was pitch black, the rain streamed down in torrents and the wind howled and gusted until the windows creaked and rattled. The whole family was sitting round the fire when suddenly there came three loud raps at the window. The man went to the door to see who was there, and found an enormous white bear.

'Good evening,' said the bear.

'Good evening,' said the man.

'Will you let me have your youngest daughter to be my wife?' asked the bear. 'If you will, I can make you as rich as now you are poor.'

The man was pleased at the thought, but said he must first speak to his daugher. So he returned to the fire and said, 'There is a great white bear outside, who promises to make me as rich as now I am poor, if my youngest daughter will go with him as his bride.' But the girl said no, and would have nothing to do with it. The man went outside again and spoke kindly to the bear, telling him to return on the following Thursday evening.

The man and his wife tried hard to persuade their daughter, telling her of the riches that would be hers. At last she gave in, washed the few rags she possessed, dressed herself as neatly as she could and made ready for the journey.

When the bear returned on the following Thursday evening she was waiting for him with her bundle. She climbed up on to his back and they were away. After they had covered some miles, the bear asked, 'Are you afraid?'

'Not in the slightest,' she replied.

On and on they went, far through the dark night, until at last they came to a towering cliff. The bear knocked, and a door opened, admitting them to a great castle. They passed through brilliantly lit rooms, gleaming with gold and silver, until they reached a long hall, in which stood a table laden with sumptuous dishes. Here the bear handed the girl a tiny silver bell, saying, 'If you want anything at all, just ring this bell.'

After she had eaten and drunk the girl felt tired and decided to go to bed, so she rang the little bell.

Immediately a door opened to reveal a room, in which stood a delicately carved bed, with silken sheets and pillows and a gold-fringed canopy. She blew out the candle and lay down to sleep. A few moments later someone entered the room and lay beside her. This happened night after night, but the girl was never able to see who it was, for he never came before the light was snuffed, and always left before dawn each morning.

For a time the girl lived in this way, quite happy and contented. But at length she began to long for her parents and her brothers and sisters, and became silent and mournful. The bear asked her one day why she was so silent and downcast.

'Alas!' she replied. 'If only I could see my parents and my brothers and sisters again.'

'That can be arranged,' said the bear, 'but you must promise me faithfully never to speak with your mother alone, but only when others are present. She will try to draw you aside into another room, but if you give way to her you will make us both most unhappy.'

On Sunday the bear took her on his back and off they went. After they had travelled a long, long way, they came to a great white castle. Before it she saw her brothers and sisters playing. Everything was so splendid that it was a joy to behold.

'This is where your parents live now,' said the bear, 'but do not forget what I told you!'

'No, I will not forget,' replied the girl, and entered the castle. The bear turned and went away.

The parents were overjoyed to see their youngest daughter again and could hardly thank her enough for all she had done for them by agreeing to go with the bear.

'But how are you enjoying your new life?' they asked.

'All goes well with me,' she replied. 'I have everything I could possibly want.'

That afternoon, as the bear had foretold, the girl's mother tried to draw her aside into a separate room to talk. 'No,' said the girl, remembering the bear's warning, 'whatever we have to say can be said in front of the rest of the family.'

I do not quite know how it came about, but before her visit was over her mother succeeded in talking to her alone. The girl told her mother that each night, when she snuffed out the light, a man came and slept beside her, but that she had never set eyes on him, for he was always away before daylight. This saddened her, for she would so dearly have liked to see him, and the days were so long and lonely by herself.

'I am sure it must be a troll,' said her mother. 'Take my advice. Wait till he is sound asleep, and then light the candle and have a good look at him. But take good care not to drop any candle grease on him!'

That evening the bear came and fetched the girl away. Before they had gone far, he asked her if things had not turned out as he had warned.

'Yes,' she admitted, for she could not lie to him.

'Do not heed your mother's advice,' he warned, 'or you will make both of us unhappy.'

'No, indeed,' she replied, 'I promise to be very careful.'

When they arrived at the castle in the cliff, the girl lay down to sleep, and as before, when she had blown out the light, the man came and lay down beside her. She waited till he was fast asleep, and then got out of bed and lit the candle. There in her bed she saw the most handsome young man she had ever set eyes on, and she so loved him that she could not resist the temptation to bend over and kiss him. But she was careless and let three drops of hot candle grease fall on his shirt so that he awoke with a start.

'What have you done?' he cried, as he opened his eyes. 'Now you have ruined our happiness. If only you could have waited for a whole year, you would have saved me! I was bewitched by my step-mother, and I must spend the hours of daylight as a bear and can become my true self only during the hours of darkness. But now it is all over between us. I must leave you and return to her. She lives in a castle which lies east of the sun and west of the moon, and there she will force me to marry a princess with a nose that is three ells long!'

The poor girl burst into tears, but it was too late: he had no choice but to go. She begged to be allowed to go with him, but he said that could not be.

'Can you not at least tell me the way, so that I may look for you?' she asked in despair.

'Yes, you can try,' he replied, 'but there is no road that will lead you there. My step-mother's castle lies east of the sun and west of the moon. I fear you will never be able to reach it.'

When the girl awoke next morning both the young man and the castle had vanished, and she found herself on the bare earth in the heart of a thick, dark wood, with her poor bundle lying beside her. She rubbed the sleep from her eyes and cried till she could cry no more. Then she set out in search of the castle and wandered for many days, until she came at last to a high mountain. At the foot of the mountain sat an old woman playing with a golden apple.

'Can you show me the way to a castle which lies east of the sun and west of the moon?' she asked. 'A prince lives there, and he must marry a princess with a nose that is three ells long.'

'How do you know him?' asked the old woman. 'Are you perhaps the girl he wanted to marry?'

'Yes,' she replied. 'I am.'

'Ah! So you are the one!' said the woman. 'Then I should like to help you, my child, but all I know about the castle is that it lies east of the sun and west of the moon, and I fear you will never find it. But I will lend you my horse to take you to my nearest neighbour, who may be able to show you the way. When you reach her, slap the horse below the left ear and send it home to me. And take this golden apple with you – you may find it useful.'

The girl thanked the old woman, mounted the horse and rode for a long, long time. At last she came to a mountain at the foot of which sat an old woman with a golden spool. The girl asked her if she could tell her the way to the castle which lay east of the sun and west of the moon.

'I doubt if you will ever get there,' she said. 'But I will lend you my horse to take you to my nearest neighbour, who may be able to tell you the way. When you reach her, just slap the animal below the left ear and send it home to me. And take this golden spool with you – you may find it useful.'

The girl mounted the horse and rode for many days and weeks. At last she came to a mountain at the foot of which sat an old woman spinning with a golden distaff. Once again she asked the way to the castle which lay east of the sun and west of the moon.

'Are you the girl the prince wanted to marry?' asked the old woman.

'Yes,' the girl replied.

But the old woman knew the way no better than the other two. 'East of the sun and west of the moon,' she repeated. 'I fear you will never find it. But I will lend you my horse to take you to the East Wind – he may be able to help you. When you reach him, just slap the horse below the left ear, and send him back to me. And take this golden distaff with you – you may find it useful.'

The girl rode on and on and on, until she arrived at the East Wind's dwelling. She lost no time in asking if he could tell her the way to the castle which lay east of the sun and west of the moon.

'Oh yes, I have heard of the prince, and the castle, too,' said the East Wind, 'but I cannot tell you the way, for I have never been so far. Let me take you to my brother the West Wind – he is much stronger than I. Perch yourself on my back and I will take you there.'

The girl jumped on to his back and off they went. When they reached the West Wind's dwelling the East Wind said that he had brought the girl whom the prince wanted to marry, and asked whether the West Wind could tell her the way to the castle which lay east of the sun and west of the moon.

'No,' said the West Wind. 'I have never blown so far. But, if you like, jump on my back and I will take you to my brother the South Wind. He is far stronger than I and blows far and wide.'

The girl jumped on to his back and it was not long before they reached the South Wind's dwelling. The West Wind lost no time in asking whether his brother knew the way to the castle which lay east of the sun and west of the moon, for the prince wanted to marry the girl he had brought with him.

'Indeed!' exclaimed the South Wind, but he did not know the way. 'I have blown far in my life-time, but I have never blown as far as that. But if you like,' he added, 'I will gladly take you to my brother the North

Wind. He is the oldest and most powerful of us all, and if he cannot tell you the way I am sure no one can.'

The girl leapt on to his back and away they blew in such a gust that the earth trembled. In next to no time they arrived at the dwelling of the North Wind. But he was so wild and blustering that he hurled a blizzard of swirling snow and ice at them when he saw them approaching.

'What do you want with me?' he shouted in a voice which made their blood run cold.

'That is a fine way to greet your brother,' exclaimed the South Wind. 'I have brought a young girl to see you. She needs your help, for she is the girl who should marry the prince who lives in the castle east of the sun and west of the moon. She wants to ask if you know the way.'

'Yes, yes, of course I know the way,' said the North Wind. 'I once blew an aspen leaf there. The effort so exhausted me that I could not blow for weeks afterwards. But, if you are not afraid and are set upon going, I will take you on my back and see if I can blow you there.'

'Yes, I am determined to reach the castle,' said the girl, 'no matter what dangers beset us.'

'Then you must spend the night here,' said the North Wind, 'for we must have a whole day before us if we are to make the attempt.'

Early next morning the North Wind wakened her and blew himself up to such an enormous size that he was quite terrifying to see.

Then off they roared with a blast which seemed as if it would hurl them right to the end of the world. In the mighty hurricane whole villages and forests were destroyed. Across wide tracts of land and sea they raged, until it seemed they could go no further. At last the

North Wind began to grow so weak that he scarcely had the strength to blow, and he sank deeper and deeper, until the waves were lapping about the girl's feet.

'Are you afraid?' he asked her.

'Not at all,' she replied.

By now they were not far from land, and the North Wind had just enough strength to set the girl down on the shore below the windows of the castle which lay east of the sun and west of the moon. The wind was so weak and exhausted that he had to rest for many days before he could journey home.

On the following morning the girl sat on the grass beneath the castle window and played with her golden apple. The first person to notice her was the long-nosed princess who was to marry the prince. 'What will you take in exchange for your golden apple?'

'It is not for sale,' replied the girl. 'Neither for gold nor silver.'

'Well, if you will not sell it for gold or silver,' said the princess, 'is there anything else you will take for it? I will give you whatever you ask.'

'You shall have it if I may sleep for one night in the prince's room,' said the girl.

'But of course you may!' exclaimed the princess, and took the golden apple.

When the girl entered the prince's room she found him deep in such a heavy sleep that she could not wake him, though she called him and shook him, and wept and cried. In the morning, as it was growing light, the long-nosed princess came and chased her out.

Again the girl sat down on the grass below the window and began to wind and thread on her golden spool. The long-nosed princess saw it, and asked the girl what she would take for it. 'It is not for sale, either for gold or silver. But, if I may spend another night in the prince's room, you shall have it.'

'Done!' said the long-nosed princess, and claimed the golden spool. But once again the girl found the prince so sound asleep that no amount of shaking and crying could rouse him. And in the morning, as it was growing light, the long-nosed princess again came and chased her out.

This time the girl sat on the grass below the window and spun with her golden distaff. When the long-nosed princess saw it she was filled with envy. She threw open the window and asked the girl if she would sell it. As before the girl answered, 'I will not sell it for gold or silver. But, if I may spend one more night in the prince's room, you shall have it.'

But some of the castle servants who slept near the prince's bedroom, had heard for two nights the weeping and wailing of a woman coming from his room, and they had told the prince about it. So, when the long-nosed princess brought him his soup on the third evening, the prince pretended to drink, but poured it away behind him, for he guessed it contained a sleeping draught. That night, when the girl entered his room, she found him wide awake and overjoyed to see her. She told him all that had happened to her and how she had reached the castle.

'You have come at just the right time,' he declared, 'for tomorrow I am to be married to the princess. But what do I care for her – you are the only one I wish to marry! So I shall tell everyone that I want to see how clever my bride is, and shall insist that she washes the three spots of candle grease out of my shirt. She will agree to do it, but I know she is bound to fail, for these drops of grease can be removed only by a Christian hand

– not by the hands of one of such a pack of trolls as owns this castle. I shall refuse to marry anyone who cannot remove the spots of grease, and when all the others have tried and failed I shall call you to try.'

Next morning when the wedding was about to take place the prince said, 'First I should like to see how clever my bride is. See, I have here a fine white shirt which I should like to wear for my wedding, but it is spotted with these three drops of candle-grease. I have decided, therefore, to marry none but the girl who can wash out the grease.'

'What is so difficult about that?' murmured all the women.

The long-nosed princess set about washing the shirt, but the longer she scrubbed, the bigger and blacker the stains became.

'You're no good at it,' declared the old troll woman, her mother. 'Give it to me.' But no sooner had she laid hands on the shirt than it grew dirtier, and the more she rubbed and rinsed, the bigger the spots became. Then all the other troll women tried to wash the shirt, but the longer they washed, the filthier it grew. And finally the whole shirt looked as though it had been hung up in the chimney.

'Not one of you is any use,' declared the prince. 'But I see a poor beggar girl below the castle window. Perhaps she knows more about washing than all of you put together. Come on in!' he called. And when the girl came up he asked her, 'Can you wash this shirt clean?'

'I do not know,' said the girl, 'but I think I can.' She took the shirt and began to wash, and in her hands it became as white as driven snow – and even whiter.

'You are my true bride!' exclaimed the prince.

The old troll mother was so angry that she burst with

57

rage; and the long-nosed princess and the whole pack of trolls must have exploded too, for I have heard nothing of them from that day to this.

The princess and his bride set free all the prisoners who had been held in the castle; and then they took as much gold and silver as they could carry and left far, far behind them the castle which lay east of the sun and west of the moon. How did they travel, and where did they go? That I do not know, but if they are the couple I think they are, they do not live far from here.

Wali Dad the Simple

There was once a poor old man called Wali Dad, who had no one in the world, neither wife nor children, and he lived by himself in a miserable little hut somewhere in the vast plains of India. Day after day he would go into the jungle to cut grass, which he would dry and sell as fodder for horses. He was a frugal old man and needed nothing but a little rice to eat, and so every day he managed to save half an anna, which he would throw into an earthenware chatti which he kept concealed in a hole in the floor.

One evening as he was finishing his scanty meal, he suddenly thought he would count his savings. With some difficulty he hauled the chatti from its hole in the floor, tipped the contents out on the table and stared in astonishment at the shining heap of coins.

What on earth could he do with all that money, he wondered. It did not occur to him to spend it on himself, for he was quite happy to spend the rest of his days as he had always done. So he flung the coins into an old sack, pushed it under his bed, and lay down to sleep.

Early the next morning he got up, slung the sack over his shoulder and staggered into the next town to a jeweller's shop, where he exchanged the money for a beautiful bangle of gold. He wrapped it carefully in his cummerbund and set out to visit a rich friend of his, a merchant who travelled about in many lands with his caravan of camels. Wali Dad was fortunate to find him at home, and after they had greeted one another and chatted about this and that, he asked his merchant friend if he could tell him who was the most beautiful and most virtuous woman he had ever come across on his travels.

After barely a moment's hesitation the merchant replied, 'The Princess of Khaistan. The renown of her beauty, her virtue and her generosity has spread far and wide.'

'Well,' said Wali Dad, 'if you should visit Khaistan again on your travels, give her this golden bangle, with the most humble greetings of an old man in whose eyes kindness and goodness are worth more than all the riches in the world.'

With these words he took the bangle out of his cummerbund and handed it to his friend. The merchant was more than a little surprised, but he promised to carry out Wali Dad's instructions.

Soon after this the merchant set out on his travels once more, and after a time he came to the city where the princess lived. As soon as the opportunity presented itself he went to the palace and had the bangle delivered to the princess, laid in a beautiful, sweet-smelling box which he himself had provided. Nor did he forget to pass on Wali Dad's message to the princess. She could not imagine who could have honoured her with such a beautiful gift but she sent her servants to tell the merchant that she would be ready to send an answer as soon as he had finished his business in the city.

After a few days had elapsed the merchant returned to the palace, and the princess gave him a camel-load of costly silks as a present for Wali Dad, together with some money for himself. The merchant set out at once on the homeward journey.

It was some time before he reached his home, but as soon as he did so he went to see Wali Dad, to give him the princess's gift. The good old man was astonished to see a camel-load of silk rolling in at his door. What could he do with such luxuries? After a little thought he asked the merchant whether he knew of a young and noble prince who might be able to put his treasure to use.

'Yes, of course,' replied the merchant immediately. 'Of all the princes I know, from Delhi to Baghdad, there is none more noble or more worthy than the young Prince of Nekabad.'

'Excellent,' exclaimed Wali Dad. 'Then take him the silk, with the blessings of an old man.' He was happy to be rid of his treasure.

The merchant's very next journey took him to Nekabad, and after he had conducted his business in the city he requested an audience with the prince. When he was admitted into the royal presence he spread the magnificent silks at the prince's feet, and asked him to accept them as the gift of an old man who valued the prince's greatness and merit. The prince was moved by such generosity, and sent for twelve of his most beautiful stud-horses, for which his country was famous, and asked the merchant to present them to Wali Dad on his behalf.

At the same time he gave the merchant a princely reward for his services.

The merchant hurried home and went straight to Wali Dad's little hut. When the old man saw the horses coming, he thought to himself, 'What luck! A whole troop of horses! They will eat cartloads of grass, and I shall be able to sell all I have without bothering to take it to the market.' And he hurried out to the edge of the jungle and started to cut grass as fast as he could.

When he returned, laden with as much grass as he could carry, he heard to his astonishment that the horses were his own. At first he stood perplexed, not knowing what to do, but then he had a sudden brainwave. He gave two horses to the merchant, and asked him to take the other ten to the Princess of Khaistan, who would doubtless find a use for such superb animals.

The merchant agreed with a laugh to do as his old friend wished, and took the horses to the princess's court. This time the princess wanted to know more about the

man who was sending her such costly gifts. Now, the merchant was most certainly an honourable man, but he hardly dared to describe Wali Dad as he really was – a wizened old man who earned a few annas each day and had hardly a rag to cover his back. So he told the princess that his friend had heard so much about her beauty and goodness that his heart moved him to lay the best things he possessed at her feet.

The princess had no idea how she should most fittingly respond to a man who showered such rich gifts upon her, so she took her father into her confidence and asked his advice.

'You cannot send his gifts back to him,' he replied. 'I think the best thing will be for you to send him so priceless a gift in return that he will be quite unable to match it. Then he will be ashamed, and will trouble you no more.' He ordered his servants to load twenty mules with silver, two mules for each of the ten horses, and to deliver them to the merchant, saying they were the princess's gift to Wali Dad.

So the merchant found himself suddenly in charge of a gleaming caravan. He had to take an armed guard with him to protect the caravan against robbers and marauding tribesmen, and it was a relief to him when he finally arrived at Wali Dad's little hut.

'Wonderful!' cried Wali Dad when he saw the treasures before his door. 'Now I can reply fittingly to the gift of the magnificent horses the prince sent me. But you, my friend,' he said to the merchant, 'you must have had to spend a great deal. If you will take six of these mules, together with their loads, and take the rest straight to Nekabad, I should be most grateful.'

The merchant was well aware that he was being most richly rewarded for his pains and agreed to set out for

Nekabad immediately, for he was curious to see what course this strange affair would take.

This time the prince reacted as the princess had done. He was at a loss to understand why a complete stranger should send him such a rich gift. He asked the merchant what sort of a person Wali Dad really was, and in order to make his story ring true, the merchant could only praise Wali Dad's virtues so highly that the old man would certainly not have recognized himself, had he been present.

Just as the King of Khaistan had done, the prince made up his mind to send his unknown benefactor so kingly a gift that he would desist from sending further presents. So he had made ready a caravan of twenty pure-bred Arab horses with gold-embroidered bridles and silver saddles, twenty of his best camels, which could travel the whole day without tiring, and twenty elephants with pearl-embroidered silken covers and silver howdahs; and this great procession of animals was to be accompanied by a troop of men. What a fine sight it was, as they streamed across country.

When Wali Dad saw from afar the dust-cloud which this immense caravan raised, he said to himself, 'Here comes a great army of men, and elephants too! I shall be glad to sell all my grass to them!' And he ran to the jungle and cut grass as fast as he could. When he returned to his hut with the first load he found the enormous caravan and the merchant, who could hardly wait to show him the magnificent train and congratulate him on his vast fortune.

'Fortune!' cried Wali Dad. 'What can an ugly old man like me, with one foot in the grave, do with a fortune? Take it to the beautiful young princess – she would be able to enjoy all these beautiful things. Keep two horses, two camels and two elephants for yourself, with all their bits and bobs – and take the rest to her.'

At first the merchant made excuses and pointed out to Wali Dad that these journeys as messenger were causing him embarrassment. Certainly he was being richly awarded for his pains, but he was tired of deceiving people. But the old man was so persistent that at last he relented. However, he determined not to let himself in for such an undertaking ever again.

After a few days' rest the great caravan set out for Khaistan. When the king saw the glittering train of animals streaming into the court-yard of his palace he was so amazed that he went down in person to see what it meant. When he heard that this was yet another present from Wali Dad to his daughter he scarcely knew what to say. He hastened to the princess's apartments and said, 'There seems little doubt, my dear, that this man is set upon marrying you. We have no alternative but to pay him a visit. He must be a man of immense wealth. And as he is so devoted to you there seems little reason why you should not marry him.'

The princess agreed, and orders were issued to make ready a great train of elephants and camels, with silken tents and banners, litters for the ladies-in-waiting and horses for the men, for the king and his daughter were to honour the noble and generous Prince Wali Dad with a visit. The merchant was to guide the procession.

The poor merchant was now in a dire predicament! He was sorely tempted to run away, but as Wali Dad's ambassador he was received with such deference and hospitality in the royal court of Khaistan that he was never alone for a moment, and so found no opportunity to escape. After a few days he realized that he would have to submit to his fate, and only hoped that some act of providence would show him a way out of this awkward and embarrassing situation.

On the seventh day the royal procession set out, to the blare of trumpets and thunderous salutes from the palace guns. Day by day they drew nearer to Wali Dad's humble abode, and with each day the poor merchant felt more and more miserable. He wondered what kind of death the king would mete out to him, and suffered inward torture. Night after night he lay awake in his bed, racking his brains for a way out.

At last they were only one day's march from Wali Dad's hut, and the merchant was sent on ahead to warn Wali Dad of the approach of the king and princess with their train.

Wali Dad was busy preparing his meagre meal of onions and stale bread when the merchant arrived and told him what had happened. Wali Dad was so overcome with confusion that he burst into tears and began to tear his white hair. He implored the merchant to hold back the royal procession for one more day.

As soon as the merchant had departed it seemed clear to Wali Dad that there was only one way out of the disgrace and despair he had brought on himself through his simplicity, and that was to take his own life.

Without saying a word to anyone about it, he went at midnight to a high cliff, at the foot of which the river wound through a deep gorge, and decided to throw himself down into the depths. When he reached the spot he walked a few steps back, took a run, and – came to a sudden halt on the very edge of the gloomy chasm. No, he could not do it!

Far beneath him, invisible in the darkness, he heard the water foaming and thundering over the rocks. The wind whistled mournfully through the gorge, and an owl fluttered and cried, 'Hoo! hoo!' close to his face. Terror-stricken, the old man shrank back from the edge of the abyss. He was frightened. Shuddering, he buried his face in his hands and began to weep loudly.

Suddenly he became aware of a soft, gleaming light flooding about him. Surely it could not be morning already? He took his hands from his face and saw two beings of unearthly beauty standing before him. They were spirits from Paradise.

'Why are you crying, old man?' asked one of them, in a voice as clear and sweet as the nightingale's.

'I am crying for shame,' he replied.

'What are you doing here?' asked the other.

'I came here to die,' he replied simply, and he told his story.

The first spirit approached him and laid a gentle hand on his shoulder, and Wali Dad felt as if something strange – he could not say what – was happening to him. His ragged old clothes were transformed into a beautiful embroidered robe, on his bare feet appeared soft, warm sandals and on his head a turban adorned with precious stones. About his neck hung a golden chain, and the old bent sickle, which he had to cut grass with for years and which hung from his belt, was suddenly changed into a gleaming sword with an ivory handle.

He stood bewildered, as in a dream, until the second spirit motioned to him to look round. What did he see? Before him a castle gate stood wide open and they walked forward along an avenue of huge plane trees. At the end of the avenue towered a magnificent palace, glowing with a thousand lights. On all the balconies and terraces servants hurried to and fro. The sentries strode up and down and saluted him respectfully as he approached. Wali Dad stood as though he had been struck dumb.

'Do not be afraid!' said one of the spirits. 'Enter into your house. Know that Allah rewards the simple and pure in heart.' With these words the two spirits vanished, leaving him alone.

Wali Dad went on, still as in a dream, and entered a great room more beautiful than any he had ever seen. Here he lay down to rest.

At first light he awoke and saw that the palace, the servants and all his fine clothes were reality, and knew that he had not dreamt it all.

Even more amazed than Wali Dad himself was the merchant, who came to him soon after sunrise. He told Wali Dad how he had lain sleepless all night, and had set out to see him at first light. But though he had searched he had been unable to find him. A great tract of thick jungle had been transformed overnight into beautiful gardens and parks. And if some of Wali Dad's servants had not found him and brought him into the palace he would have believed that he had gone mad and was imagining it all.

After Wali Dad had related all that had taken place that night the merchant hurried to the princess and the King of Khaistan, to conduct them to the palace.

The feasting in honour of the royal visitors from Khaistan lasted for three days and three nights. Every evening the king and his courtiers ate from golden plates and drank from golden goblets, and at the end of each meal the guests were asked to take the plates and goblets home with them as a token of remembrance. There had never been such a grand and glorious feast.

On the fourth day the King of Khaistan took Wali
Dad aside and asked him if he wished to marry his
daughter. Wali Dad replied that he would not have
dared to dream of such an honour – he was far too old
and ugly for such a beautiful young woman. However,
he asked the king to stay on at the palace until he could
send for his friend the Prince of Nekabad.

The king promised to do so, and next day Wali Dad

sent the merchant to Nekabad with so many rich gifts that the prince could hardly refuse to come. As soon as he set eyes on the princess the prince fell head over heels in love with her, and they were married at once in Wali Dad's palace. There has never been, before or since, a grander or more sumptuous marriage feast.

When the celebrations were over the prince took his bride back to Nekabad, and the king rode home to Khaistan. Wali Dad lived on for many years and showed infinite kindness to all who were in need. And he always remained as simple and kind-hearted as he had been as a poor grass-cutter.

The Frog Prince or Iron Henry

In olden times when wishes sometimes came true there lived a king whose daughters were all beautiful, but the youngest one was so lovely that even the sun, who has seen most things, was dazzled by her. Not far from the king's castle lay a dense forest, and in the forest at the foot of an old lime tree was a well. On warm days the youngest princess would go out into the shade of the forest to sit at the edge of the well. When she was bored she would play with a golden ball, throwing it high into the air and catching it again. It was her favourite game.

One day she missed the golden ball when it came down. It bounced on the ground and rolled straight into the well. Now the well was deep, very deep, so that it was impossible to see the bottom, and the princess's ball was lost from sight. She began to cry as if her heart would break.

In the midst of her sobbing, someone called to her, 'Why are you crying, princess? Your weeping would make even a stone take pity on you!'

She looked round to see where the voice was coming from and saw a frog, stretching its fat, ugly head out of the water. 'Oh, it's you, you old water-splasher!' she said. 'I'm crying because my golden ball has fallen into the well.'

'Be quiet, then, and don't cry,' replied the frog. 'I will help you. But what will you give me if I bring your plaything up to you?'

'Whatever you wish, dear frog,' she said. 'My clothes,

my pearls and precious stones, and even the golden crown from my head. You can have them all.'

'Your clothes, your pearls and precious stones and your golden crown are of no use to me,' replied the frog. 'But if you will love me and let me be your companion and playfellow, if you will let me sit with you at table and eat from your golden plate and drink from your little golden cup, if you will let me sleep in your bed – if you will promise me all these things, then I will dive down and fetch your golden ball for you.'

'Of course,' she said. 'I will promise you anything you like if you will bring back my ball.' But she thought: What strange things that silly frog says. He sits and croaks in the water with the other frogs. How can he be a companion to a human?

The frog dived down and a few moments later re-appeared, bearing in his mouth the golden ball, which he threw into the grass.

The princess was delighted when she saw her beautiful ball. She picked it up and ran off with it.

'Wait! Wait!' called the frog. 'Take me with you. I cannot run as fast as you!' But his desperate croaking was all in vain for she paid him no heed. She hurried home and had soon forgotten the poor frog, who returned sadly to his well.

The following day when the king and all his courtiers were sitting down at table, eating from their golden plates, something came creeping, splish-splash, splish-splash, up the great marble staircase. When it reached the top there came a knock at the door and a voice called, 'Youngest princess, open the door for me!'

She ran to see who was there, but when she saw the frog sitting outside she hastily slammed the door. She took her place at the table again, but everyone could see that she was upset and frightened.

The king saw how fast her heart was beating, and said, 'My child, why are you so frightened? What is the matter? Has an ogre come to fetch you?

'No, no,' she replied, 'it is not an ogre, but a loathsome frog.'

'What does the frog want of you?'

'My dear father, yesterday when I was playing with my ball in the forest it fell down a well, and because I was crying so much the frog dived down and brought it back to me. Because he was so insistent I promised that he could be my playfellow. But I never thought he could leave the water. Now he is outside and wants to come in.'

The knocking came a second time, and a voice cried:

'Princess, youngest princess,
        open to me!
Do you not remember
        what you promised yesterday
        by the waters of the well?
Princess, youngest princess,
        open to me!'

Then the old king said, 'If you made a promise, you must keep it. Go and open the door for him.'

She went and opened the door. The frog hopped into the room and followed close behind her, up to her chair. There he sat, and croaked, 'Lift me up beside you!' She hesitated, until her father ordered her to keep her promise. As soon as the frog was on the chair he wanted to be on the table, and when he was there he said, 'Now just

move your little golden plate nearer to me, so that we can both eat together.'

She did as he asked, but it was easy to see that she did not do it willingly.

The frog seemed to enjoy his food, but every bite the princess took seemed to stick in her throat. When the meal was over the frog said, 'I have eaten well and now I am tired. Take me up to your room and make the bed ready, and we will take a rest.' The princess began to cry, for she was frightened of the cold frog.

The king grew angry then, and said, 'You have no right to despise anyone who helped you when you were in need.' So she picked up the frog between her forefinger and thumb, took him to her room and set him down in a corner. As soon as she had lain down on the bed, the frog crawled to the bedside and said, 'I am tired. I want to sleep as well as you. Lift me up beside you or I will tell your father!'

The princess was furious with the frog. She picked him up and flung him with all her might against the wall. 'Perhaps that will keep you quiet, you loathsome frog!'

But what fell to the ground was no frog, but a handsome prince with beautiful, smiling eyes, who said, 'I was under the curse of a wicked witch, and no one could free me from the well but you. We will return to my kingdom tomorrow.' Then they fell asleep.

When the first rays of the rising sun woke them the following morning, eight white horses came trotting up the palace drive, drawing a magnificent carriage. White ostrich feathers bobbed on their heads and the bridles were chains of pure gold. At the reins stood faithful Henry, the prince's servant. Henry had been so miserable when his master had been turned into a frog that he had had three iron hoops bound round his chest, to prevent his heart from breaking.

Faithful Henry had brought the carriage to take his master back to his own kingdom. He helped the prince and princess in and took up the reins, full of joy at his lord's deliverance. Before they had gone far the prince heard a loud crack, as though something had broken, and he cried out, 'Henry, the carriage is breaking!'

'No, my lord, it is not the carriage, but one of the hoops from my heart, which was in danger of breaking all the time you were a frog squatting in the well!'

There was another loud crack and another, and each time the prince thought that the carriage must be falling apart. But it was only the hoops bursting joyfully from faithful Henry's heart, because his master was happy and free once more.

Beauty and the Beast

There was once a prosperous merchant who had six children – three boys and three girls. As he was a highly intelligent man himself, he insisted on all his children being well educated, and he engaged the very best tutors for them.

His daughters were all beautiful, but by far the loveliest was the youngest, who had been called Beauty from her earliest childhood. Truth to tell, her sisters were jealous of her because she had not grown out of the name. Besides, Beauty was more gentle and kind-hearted than her sisters, who were arrogant because of their great wealth. They liked to pretend they were great ladies and spurned the friendship of other merchants' daughters. They desired more select company. Day after day they would go dancing, to the theatre, or walking in the park, and they mocked their young sister, who spent most of her time reading good books.

Since it was well known how wealthy the family was, the sons of other wealthy merchants sought the three daughters in marriage. But the two elder sisters rejected them scornfully, vowing they would marry no less than a duke or a count.

But then the merchant lost his entire fortune, and all that remained was a tiny cottage in the country, miles away from the city. In tears he explained to his children what had happened and told them they must be prepared to work in the fields. At first the two elder sisters refused, saying that they still had a great many willing suitors in spite of their poverty. But they were mistaken

for none of their former suitors would have anything to do with them now that they were poor. Indeed, many were delighted that their pride and arrogance had been punished. 'They do not deserve to be pitied. Let them look after the sheep and still try to look like grand ladies,' they said.

At the same time, everyone was sorry for Beauty. 'What a dear, kind child she is! How good she was to all the poor people, how friendly and how gentle!' And, indeed, a great many young noblemen still wished to marry her even though she had not a penny to her name. But she always answered that she could not possibly desert her father in his misfortune; she would go with him to the country, to comfort him and help him in his work.

She was sad for her father's sake that all their money had gone, but she knew that no amount of crying would bring it back, and that it was quite possible to be really happy without great wealth or rich possessions.

In the country the man and his children worked hard in the fields to make a living. Beauty would get up at four in the morning to tidy the house and make breakfast. In the evenings, when the day's work was done, she would play the piano or sing as she worked at her spinning-wheel. The two elder sisters, on the other hand, were bored to death. They never got up before ten in the morning, never did a stroke of work on the farm, and spent all day lamenting their lost wealth and their fine clothes. 'Just look at our sister!' they exclaimed. 'That she can be happy in such miserable surroundings shows how stupid and vulgar she must be!'

Their good father, however, marvelled that Beauty was so patient with her two sisters, for not only did they leave her all the work to do, but they were ceaselessly scolding her and finding fault.

After the family had been living in solitude in the country for about a year, the merchant suddenly received a letter which told him that one of his ships had at long last come home to port safe and sound with all its cargo on board. The two elder sisters were overjoyed at the news, for they thought that they would now be able to leave the country, where they had been so bored. As their father made ready to set out for the port, they asked him to bring them dresses, furs, hats and all sorts of finery. Beauty did not ask for anything, for she knew that the sale of the whole cargo would not pay for half of what her two sisters demanded. 'Aren't you going to ask me to buy you anything, Beauty?' said her father.

'How good and kind you are to think of me,' she replied. 'May I ask you to bring me a rose, for we have none growing here?'

The merchant rode on his way; but when he reached the port he discovered that his goods just sufficed to pay his debts and no more. So he returned home as poor as when he had set out.

He had only thirty miles to go and was already looking forward to seeing his children again, when he lost his way in a great forest he was crossing. It was snowing heavily and the wind blew in such gusts that twice he was blown from his horse. As night had already fallen he was afraid he might die of cold and hunger, or that he might even be attacked by the wolves which he heard howling all round him in the darkness. But then he caught sight of a light twinkling at the end of a long avenue of trees. He pressed on towards it and found that it came from a brilliantly lit castle. The merchant uttered a heart-felt prayer of thanks and hurried forward to investigate. To his astonishment he found not a soul inside, although all the lights were blazing. No one answered his shouts, and his horse – seeing an empty stable – trotted into it and helped itself eagerly to the hay and oats. The merchant went from room to room, but there was no one there. He came to a great hall where a huge fire blazed in the hearth and a table stood laden with roast meats, but with only one place laid.

The rain and snow had soaked the merchant to the skin, so he stood in front of the fire to dry himself and wait for the master of the house to appear. When the clock struck eleven and still no one had come, he decided he could wait no longer. Trembling, he helped himself to some roast chicken and a glass of wine. Emboldened by the food and warmth, he went through several more rooms, all magnificently furnished. Then he came to a bedroom with a fine, soft bed. It was past midnight and

78

he was exhausted, so he closed the door and lay down to sleep.

He did not wake until ten the following morning, and when he rose he was astonished to find a fresh cloak in place of his old, threadbare one. 'Clearly this castle belongs to some good fairy who has taken pity on me!' he said. He looked out of the window and there was no snow to be seen. Acres of flowers met his delighted gaze.

He returned to the great hall where he had eaten on the previous evening. There he found a bowl of steaming hot chocolate waiting for him, so he said aloud, 'Thank you, my good fairy, for preparing me such a fine breakfast.'

After he had drunk his chocolate, the good man went out to fetch his horse. As he passed a rose-hedge he remembered that his youngest daughter had asked him to bring her a rose, so he broke off a spray with several fine blooms on it. At once he heard a great roar and turned to see such a fearsome monster approaching that he almost fainted with fear.

'You are most ungrateful!' roared the beast. 'I saved your life by taking you into my castle in the blizzard, and now you steal my roses, which I love more than anything in the world. You shall pay for this outrage with your life! I give you fifteen minutes to say your prayers and make ready.'

The poor merchant threw himself on his knees. 'Forgive me, my lord!' he begged. 'I had no idea I would be offending you by plucking a rose for my daughter.'

'Do not call me lord,' said the beast. 'Call me monster. I do not like flattery. I will forgive you on one condition – that one of your daughters will come here to die willingly in your place. Go now, and do not try to bargain with me. But before you go you must swear to return within three months, unless one of your daughters is willing to die for you.'

The good man did not intend to sacrifice any of his daughters, but he thought at least he would like to see his family again before he died. So he swore to return.

'Now you may go,' said the beast. 'But,' he added, 'I should not like you to leave here empty-handed. In the room where you spent last night you will find an empty trunk. Put into it anything you wish, and I will have it sent after you.'

With that, the beast left him, and the poor man thought that, if he had to die, at least he would be able to leave his children something. So he returned to the room where he had spent the night. There he found any number of gold coins, and with these he filled the trunk. Then he fetched his horse from the stables and left the castle as full of sorrow as he had been full of joy when he arrived. His horse soon found a way out of the forest, and within a few hours the merchant reached his home.

His children gathered round him, but instead of rejoicing in their welcome the merchant began to weep. 'Here, Beauty,' he said as he handed her the roses, 'take these roses. They have cost your father very dear.' And he related all that had befallen him. The two elder daughters began to scold Beauty, for she had not shed a single tear at his story.

'Why should I weep for my father's death?' Beauty exclaimed. 'He shall not die. The monster is willing to accept one of us in his place, and I shall be glad to prove my love by going when the time comes.'

'I am moved by your devotion, my daughter,' said her father, 'but I will not send you to your death.'

'I assure you, father,' she replied, 'that you shall not return to the beast's castle without me. You cannot prevent my following you. How could I live without you? I would much rather be devoured by the monster than die of sorrow because of your death.'

There was nothing her father could say to dissuade her. Beauty had quite made up her mind. Her sisters were delighted, for Beauty's virtue had roused their jealousy.

The merchant was so grieved at the thought of losing his daughter that he had quite forgotten about the trunkful of gold. But, as he was about to lie down to sleep that night, he saw to his astonishment that it was standing by his bed. He decided not to tell the children how rich he had become, for then they would have wanted to return to the city, and he had resolved to end his days in the country. He revealed his secret to Beauty, however, and she told him that several young noblemen had visited them during his absence and that two of them loved her sisters. 'Do let them be married, dear father,' she implored him, for her kind heart forgave her sisters all their faults.

At the end of the three months the merchant set off once more with a heavy heart, and with him went Beauty. Towards evening they reached the castle in the forest and found it as brilliantly lit as it had been the first time. The merchant took his daughter into the great hall where he found the table set for two and laden with appetizing dishes. The poor father could not bring himself to eat, but Beauty, who took great care to appear calm, sat down at the table and set food before him.

When the meal was over they heard a terrifying roar, and in tears the merchant bade his daughter farewell, for he knew that it was the beast. Beauty could hardly conceal her trembling when she saw the frightful monster, but she was calm once more when the beast asked her if she had come willingly. 'Yes,' she replied, with only a faint quiver in her voice.

'Thank you. You are very kind,' said the creature. 'Good man,' he continued to the father, 'you must leave this place at dawn tomorrow, and on no account are you to return.' And with these words the monster vanished.

'Oh, my dear child!' exclaimed the merchant, and kissed Beauty. 'Listen to me. Leave me here to die.'

'No, Father,' replied Beauty firmly. 'Tomorrow you must go and leave me to my fate. Perhaps the beast may take pity on me.'

They went up to bed, expecting to lie awake all night.

But scarcely had they lain down than their eyes closed in a deep and peaceful sleep. Beauty had a vivid dream in which a strange woman appeared and said, 'My dear, you have a generous heart. Your kind action in giving your own life to save your father will not go unrewarded. Have no fear.'

When she awoke she told the dream to her father, and it comforted him a little as he took leave of his daughter, filled with sorrow.

Beauty sat down in the great hall and began to cry. But she was a courageous girl and she soon dried her tears, determined that she would not waste the short time remaining to her in vain regrets, for she believed the monster would devour her when evening came. She decided that she would have a good look round the beautiful castle. But how amazed she was when she came to a door with 'Beauty's Room' written upon it. She opened the door to look inside and was dazzled by the splendour of the room. But what she noticed above all was a marvellous library, a piano and a pile of music books. 'Well, they evidently do not wish me to be bored,' she said softly to herself. Then she thought that such great preparations would hardly have been made for her if she had only a day to live, and this thought cheered her.

She opened the book case, and her eye was caught by a book on which was written in gold letters: 'Wish. Command. You are queen and mistress here.' 'Oh,' she sighed, 'my only wish is to see my poor father and to know what he is doing now.' She did not speak these words aloud, but when her gaze fell on a large mirror she was astonished to see her home. Her father was coming sadly into the house and her two sisters were going to meet him. In spite of the faces they were making in their efforts to look sad and downcast, it was quite clear that they were glad to be rid of their youngest sister. Gradually the vision faded, but the castle now seemed warmer and friendlier and Beauty could not help thinking that perhaps the monster could not be so wicked.

At midday she found the table laid for her in the great hall, and as she ate she heard the most wonderful music, although there was no one to be seen.

As she was about to sit down to her evening meal she heard the roar of the monster, and she shuddered in spite of herself. 'Beauty,' he said, 'may I stay and watch while you eat?'

'You are master here,' she replied, trembling.

'No,' he replied. 'You alone are mistress here. You need only send me away if you find me a nuisance and I will leave at once. Tell me one thing – do you find me ugly?'

'I cannot lie,' answered Beauty. 'You are not beautiful, but I believe you are kind at heart.'

'You are right,' said the monster. 'But I am also stupid, for I am only a beast.'

'You cannot possibly be stupid if you think you are!' she replied. 'No simpleton ever realizes his stupidity.'

'Eat, Beauty,' said the monster, 'and try not to be bored in this house, for everything here belongs to you.'

'You are truly very kind. It seems to make you a little less ugly now that I know what a kind heart you have.'

'I may be kind-hearted,' said the monster, 'but I am still a beast.'

'There are many men who look more frightful than you,' continued Beauty, 'and I would rather have you, in spite of your appearance, than those who conceal a deceitful, selfish and ungrateful heart in a human form.'

Beauty enjoyed her meal. She had lost nearly all her fear of the monster, yet she almost died of fright when the beast said, 'Beauty, will you be my wife?'

For some moments she said nothing. She was afraid he would be angry if she refused, yet she said softly, 'No good monster, I cannot.'

The poor creature sighed so deeply that the whole castle seemed to shake. But Beauty had no cause for alarm, for the beast said, 'Good night, Beauty. Sleep well,' and left the room.

Beauty spent three peaceful months in the castle. Every evening the monster would come to her and talk very pleasantly with her during dinner. She soon became quite accustomed to his ugliness and, far from dreading the hour of his arrival, she would find herself glancing at the clock to see if it were nearly nine o'clock, for he always came at that hour.

Only one thing troubled her: every night before going to bed the monster would ask her to marry him, and he seemed overwhelmed with grief when each time she said no.

One day Beauty said to him, 'You cause me great sorrow, my monster. I should like to marry you, but I cannot honestly lead you to hope that it could ever be. But I will always be your friend – try to be content with that.'

'I have no other choice,' replied the monster. 'I know how fearsome I look, but I love you deeply. I am more than content that you will stay here with me. Promise that you will never leave me.'

Beauty blushed at these words, for she had seen in the mirror that her father lay ill with grief at losing his daughter, and she longed to see him again. 'I willingly promise never to leave you completely,' she said, 'but

I long so desperately to see my poor father again that I think I shall die if you refuse me this joy.'

'I would rather die myself than cause you grief,' said the monster. 'I will send you home to your father, and you may stay with him, even though I know I shall die of longing.'

'No, no,' said Beauty, with tears in her eyes. 'I love you far too much, and I could not bear to be the cause of your death. I will return within eight days.'

'You will be home tomorrow morning,' said the monster. 'But remember your promise. As soon as you want to come back, lay your ring on the table before you go to sleep. Goodbye, Beauty!' As usual he sighed as he left the room and Beauty retired sadly to her bed.

When she awoke next morning she found herself in her father's house, lying in her own bed. She rang the little bell at her bedside and her father hurried in. His joy knew no bounds when he saw his dear child again.

When the first flood of joy was past Beauty suddenly thought that she could hardly get up if she had no clothes. But her father discovered a big trunk in the next room, full of golden, diamond-embroidered gowns. In her heart Beauty thanked the monster for his thoughtfulness.

She rose and dressed, and in the meantime her two sisters, who had been married and now lived most unhappily with their husbands, had been sent the news of her happy return. When they saw her, radiant in her loveliness and dressed like a princess, they almost expired with envy. Although Beauty did her best to console them, their jealousy grew as she told them how happy she was. The two jealous sisters went out into the garden to conceal their annoyance, and the elder one said, 'We will keep her here longer than eight days. Her stupid monster will be so angry with her for not keeping her promise that he will be sure to devour her.'

'You are quite right,' agreed the other sister. 'But we shall have to be friendly with her if we are to succeed.'

When the eight days were up, the two sisters seemed so miserable at Beauty's impending departure that she agreed to stay for another week. And yet she reproached herself, for she knew well how the poor monster must be suffering on her account. On the tenth night she dreamt that she was in the castle garden and that the monster lay dying in the grass, reproaching her for her ingratitude. She awoke with a start and burst into tears. 'How could I be so wicked as to cause him pain! How can he help being ugly? He has a kind heart, and that means more than everything else. Why should I not marry him? I should be happier with him than my two sisters are with their husbands. It is not a man's intelligence or his good looks that make a woman happy, but his kindness and thoughtfulness.'

With these words she sat up, laid her ring on the table and then fell into a deep sleep. When she awoke next morning she found to her joy that she was once again in the monster's castle. She rose and dressed in her finest clothes to please him, and spent the whole day in desperate longing until at last it was nine o'clock. But when the hour struck, there was no sign of the monster.

Then Beauty was filled with fear that she might have caused his death. She ran sobbing through the castle, looking for the monster everywhere, until suddenly she remembered her dream. She ran to the stream in the garden, and there she found the beast lying on the ground as though dead. Without the least fear she flung herself on the body, but when she felt a flutter in the beast's heart she scooped some water from the stream and sprinkled it on his face. The monster opened his great, sad eyes and said reproachfully, 'You forgot your promise. I was so heart-broken that I came here to die.'

'No, no, my faithful beast!' sobbed Beauty. 'You must live and be my husband. I thought it was only friendship I felt towards you. How wrong I was! Now I know that I cannot possibly live without you!'

Hardly had the words left her lips than the whole castle glowed with brilliant light. The strains of sweet music and the joyful bursting of fireworks proclaimed a great feast. But Beauty had no eyes for all this splendour. She turned to her dear beast, full of concern lest he should die. But what was her surprise! He had vanished, and at her feet she saw a most handsome prince, who thanked her for having released him from enchantment. 'A wicked fairy condemned me to live as a beast,' he explained, 'until a beautiful girl would marry me. In the

whole world only you were good enough to be moved by my own heart, and even if I offer you my crown, I shall never be able to repay the debt of thanks I owe you.'

Beauty lent the handsome prince her hand to help him to his feet, and together they went into the castle. Beauty could scarcely contain her delight on finding her father and her whole family in the great hall, brought there by the strange woman who had appeared to Beauty in her dream.

'Beauty,' said the strange woman, who was a powerful fairy, 'you are now rewarded for making a good choice, in preferring goodness and kindness to beauty and intelligence. You shall be a great queen, and I hope that the throne will not destroy your good qualities. As for you, my ladies,' she said, turning to Beauty's two sisters, 'I know your hearts and the wickedness they harbour. You shall be turned into a pair of statues, but beneath the stone you shall retain your understanding. You shall stand at the gates of the palace to witness your sister's good fortune, and you shall regain your human form only when you acknowledge your faults. But I fear you will remain statues for ever. Arrogance, ill-temper, laziness and greed can all be cured – but it is a true miracle if a wicked and envious heart repents.'

In that instant the fairy raised her wand, and everyone in the hall was transported to the prince's kingdom. His subjects welcomed him, full of joy, and he and Beauty were married and lived happily together for many, many years.

Dick Whittington and his Cat

A long time ago there lived in England a little boy called Dick Whittington. His parents had both died when he was tiny. He was still too young to work for a living, so he found life very hard. He had very little to eat, and on some days he had nothing at all. The people of his village were so poor that they could spare nothing at all, except potato peelings and an occasional dry crust of bread.

Now Dick had heard many strange things about the great city of London, for in those days the country folk believed that everyone in London was wealthy, that there was music and singing all day long and that the streets were paved with gold.

One day, as Dick was standing beneath the signpost, a great coach with eight horses, all wearing bells round their necks, rolled through the village. This coach must be going to London, he thought, so he plucked up courage and asked the coachman to let him run with the coach. Learning that Dick had neither father nor mother, the coachman felt that he could hardly be worse off in London than in the village, so he told him he could come along.

So Dick came safely to London, and he was in such a hurry to see the streets paved with gold that he did not even take time to thank the coachman properly. He ran along street after street as fast as his legs would carry him, and kept on thinking that the next street he came to would be paved with gold. Back in the village Dick had three times seen a gold sovereign, and he remembered what a heap of coins they had each been changed for. And so he thought that all he would need to do to have as much money as he would ever need would be to break off a little piece of gold from the pavement.

Poor Dick ran about until he was quite exhausted. Instead of gold, all he saw in the streets of London was dirt. When darkness fell he curled up in a dark corner and cried himself to sleep.

Next morning he was ravenous. He ran from one person to another, saying, 'Please give me a ha'penny to buy a little bread.' But no one stopped to speak to him, and only two or three people gave him a ha'penny, so that poor Dick was soon weak and faint with hunger. In desperation he stopped all sorts of people to beg from them, and one of them said roughly, 'Why don't you work instead of loitering about, you idle good-for-nothing?' 'I should like to work,' replied Dick. 'May I work for you?' But the man only cursed and went on his way.

At last a kind-looking gentleman saw how hungry the boy was. 'Why don't you do some work, my lad?' he asked. 'I should like to work,' replied Dick, 'but where can I find it?' 'You can come with me and help with the haymaking, if you wish,' said the gentleman. Dick worked with a will until all the hay had been brought in, and for a while things went well.

But after the haymaking he was as badly off as before. One day, desperate with hunger, he lay down at the door of Mr Fitzwarren, a rich merchant. He was soon found there by the cook, who was always in a bad humour. She was in the middle of preparing the midday meal for the merchant and his good wife, and shouted at poor Dick, 'What are you doing there, you lazy vagabond? We have too many beggars already. If you don't move on, I'll throw the slops over you – perhaps that will make you jump.'

At that very moment Mr Fitzwarren arrived home for his meal, and when he saw the ragged, dirty boy sitting at his door, he said, 'What are you doing there, boy? You look old enough to work. You must be a lazy good-for-nothing.' 'Not at all, sir,' replied Dick. 'I am not lazy and am only too eager to do some work. But nobody will give me any, and I think I am ill with hunger.'

'Poor fellow, stand up and let me see what is the matter,' said Mr Fitzwarren. Dick tried to stand, but immediately collapsed on the ground. He had eaten nothing for three days and was too weak even to beg for halfpennies. The good merchant had him carried into the house and given a good meal. After that he was told he could stay if he helped the cook.

Little Dick would have been happy in this household if the cook had not always been in such a bad temper. 'You're always under my feet,' she grumbled continually. 'Get on and clean the spit. Then you can scrub the pots and pans, light the fire and wash up. And be quick about it!' And she would fetch him a crack on the head with the soup ladle.

At length Mr Fitzwarren's daughter Alice discovered how badly the cook was treating Dick and warned her that she would be dismissed if she was not kinder to him. So the cook began to treat him a little better, but Dick had other discomforts to bear. His bed stood in an attic whose walls and ceiling were full of holes, and every night he was tormented by rats and mice. One day a gentleman gave him a penny for cleaning his shoes, and Dick decided to buy a cat. The very next day he met a little girl with a cat and asked if she would sell it to him for a penny. 'Yes, sir,' she said, 'but it's a real bargain, for she is an excellent mouser.'

Dick hid his cat in the attic and never forgot to take her some of his food. In a very short while there was not a rat or a mouse in the attic, and Dick could sleep peacefully at night.

Not long after this his master had a ship rigged out, and it lay in the harbour, ready to set sail. As it was the custom to offer all the servants the opportunity to make their fortunes on any voyage, Mr Fitzwarren called them all into his room and asked them if they had anything they would like to have sold or exchanged for them in foreign parts. Everyone had something except poor Dick. He had neither money nor possessions and so he did not go with the others to his master's room. Alice guessed the reason and sent for him.

'I should like part of my money to be his share,' she told her father.

'That is no use,' he replied. 'It must be something of his own.'

When poor Dick heard this he said, 'I have nothing but a cat, which I bought a while ago for a penny.'

'Fetch your cat, boy, and send her along to the ship.' So Dick went up to the attic and brought the cat down. With tears in his eyes he handed her to the captain and said, 'That means no more sleep at nights because of the rats and mice.'

Everyone laughed at Dick except Alice, who was sorry for him and gave him money to buy another cat. This and many other kindnesses which Alice showed poor Dick made the cook more and more jealous of him, and she began to treat him more harshly than before. She never stopped tormenting him, reminding him of how he had sent his cat to sea. 'Do you think the cat will fetch enough money to buy a stick to beat you with?' she said.

At length Dick could stand this treatment no longer and made up his mind to run away. He packed his few possessions together and slipped away early on the morning of the first of November, All Saint's Day. But he did not get further than Holloway. Here he sat down to rest on a stone, which is called 'Whittington's Stone' to this very day, and considered which road he should take.

While he was wondering what to do, he heard Bow Bells ring out loud and clear:

Turn again, Dick Whittington,
Thrice Lord Mayor of London.

'Lord Mayor of London!' he said to himself. 'Well, why not? It is worth putting up with a great deal if I am to be Lord Mayor in the end. Then, when I am a man, I can ride in a fine coach. All right, I'll go back and bear the old cook's cuffing and scolding until I am Lord Mayor of London.' Dick went back and, luckily, was hard at work before the cook came downstairs.

But now we must follow the travels of Miss Pussy to the coast of Africa. For many a long week the ship, with the cat on board, sailed the ocean, until the winds drove it ashore on the Barbary Coast, where the Moors lived. Crowds of people came down to the shore to stare at the crew, because they were a different colour from themselves. When they had got to know the captain and his crew they eagerly bought the fine wares with which the ship was laden.

When the captain saw it, he sent a messenger with the

best goods he had to the king of the country. The king was most impressed and sent for the captain. He and his companions were given a gold and silver carpet to sit on, according to the custom of that country. The king and queen sat down to dine with them, but hardly had the food been brought in than score upon score of rats and mice appeared and in a twinkling devoured every morsel of food. The captain, in some surprise, asked the king if he did not find this plague of rats and mice very troublesome.

'Indeed, we do,' replied the king. 'I would give half my treasures to be rid of them.' The captain learned that not only did the rats and mice eat all the food, but that they worried the king at all times, even in bed at night, so that he had had to set a guard in order to be able to sleep.

The captain almost leapt for joy, suddenly remembering poor Dick Whittington and his cat. He told the king that he had an animal on board his ship that would undoubtedly rid him of the plague of rats. When the king heard it he jumped so high for joy that his turban fell off. 'Bring me this animal,' he said. 'This plague is intolerable, and if your animal can really rid me of it I will gladly fill your ship with gold and precious stones.'

The captain, who knew his business, now praised all Miss Pussy's good qualities. 'I am not sure that I really ought to let the animal go,' he said to the king, 'for my own ship will be at the mercy of rats and mice if I have no cat on board. However, I shall be glad to fetch her for you to look at, if you wish.'

'Hurry, hurry!' exclaimed the king. 'I can hardly wait to see the animal.'

The captain ran back to the ship while another meal

was being prepared. He tucked the cat under his arm, and arrived back at the palace to find the royal table seething with rats and mice. When the cat saw them she leapt from the captain's arms, and within a few moments nearly all the rats and mice lay dead, except for the few which had fled to their holes in fright.

The king was highly delighted to be rid of such a great plague so easily, and the queen asked for the cat to be brought to her so that she could see the amazing creature. So the captain called, 'Puss, puss, puss!' and took the cat over to the queen. But she took fright and drew back, not daring to touch the fearsome creature that had killed so many rats and mice.

The captain, however, stroked the cat and laid her on the princess's lap, where she played with Her Highness's fingers and then purred herself to sleep.

When the king had witnessed the heroic feats of which Miss Pussy was capable and had been told that her kittens would soon spread throughout his kingdom and keep it free of rats and mice, he bought the captain's entire cargo. But he gave ten times more for the cat than for all the cargo put together.

The captain then took his leave of the king, set sail for England with a favourable wind behind him and arrived safely in London within a few days of reaching port.

One morning, shortly after Mr Fitzwarren had entered his warehouse to begin the day's work there came a knock at his door.

'Who's there?' he asked.

'A friend, good sir,' was the prompt reply. 'I have come to bring you good news of your ship.' The merchant rose in such a hurry that he forgot all about his gout, opened the door and – who did he see? His captain with a chest full of jewels! He could hardly believe his eyes, and thanked God for granting him such a successful voyage.

The captain told him the story of the cat and showed him the rich gift which the king and queen had sent for poor Dick. Mr Fitzwarren summoned all his servants to hear the glad tidings. One of his men suggested that such a vast treasure was too much for Dick, but Mr Fitzwarren proved his honesty and fairness in his reply. 'God forbid,' he said, 'that I should take so much as a penny of what belongs to Dick.'

Then he sent for Dick, who was busy scrubbing pots and pans and was dirty from top to toe. He begged to be excused, for his master's room was clean and his shoes were dirty. But the merchant insisted on his presence.

Mr Fitzwarren had a chair brought for Dick and told him to sit down. Dick thought they were all making fun of him, and said, 'Please let me go back to my work in peace!'

'I promise you, Mr Whittington,' said his master, 'we are in no way making fun of you. I am delighted at the wonderful news which has been brought by my captain, this gentleman here. He has sold your cat to the king of the Moors, and has brought in return a treasure that far exceeds my worldly wealth. May I wish you a long and happy life in which to enjoy it.' Then he ordered his men to open the treasure chest and show Dick his fortune.

Poor Dick scarcely knew what to do in his joy. He urged his master to take as much of it as he wanted, for he owed everything to his kindness and generosity. 'No, no!' replied Mr Fitzwarren. 'This is all yours, and I am sure you will use it well.'

Dick then asked his mistress and Alice to take part of his treasure, but they would not take anything. But he was far too unselfish a boy to keep it all for himself. He made a present to the ship's captain as well as to the crew and all Mr Fitzwarren's servants, even the cantankerous cook.

Mr Fitzwarren advised him to send for a tailor without delay and to have clothes made, fit for a gentleman of his wealth. And he asked him to remain in his house as a guest for as long as he liked, until he had found a house of his own.

When Dick had washed his face, combed his hair and put on respectable clothes, he looked a remarkably handsome young man, and Alice, who had always been so kind, quickly lost her heart to him. Mr Fitzwarren saw that they loved one another and gave his consent to their marriage. The day of the wedding was soon set, and they were brought to church by the Lord Mayor of London and all the wealthy city merchants.

The story goes that Dick Whittington and his wife

lived a long and happy life and that they had seven children. Dick became city magistrate, was three times Lord Mayor of London and was knighted by Henry V.

After the conquest of France he gave such a magnificent banquet for the king and queen that the king said, 'Never has a king had such a subject.' And when Sir Richard – for so Dick was now called – heard this, he replied, 'Never has a subject had such a king.'

Until the year 1780 the statue of Sir Richard Whittington, with his cat in his arm, stood over the arched gateway of the old prison at Newgate, which he himself had built for the prisoners.

The Fir Tree

In the heart of the forest stood a pretty little fir tree, growing in a good situation. It enjoyed plenty of sunshine, and plenty of space, and round about grew a number of much taller comrades – firs and spruces. The little fir tree's one desire was to grow taller. It spared not a thought for the warm sun and fresh air, nor did it pay any attention to the farm children who passed by, chattering and laughing, in search of wild strawberries and raspberries. Often they would have a whole jar full of berries or a long row of strawberries threaded on to a straw. 'Look at the pretty little fir tree!' they would say to one another, which pleased the little fir tree not at all.

Next year the tree was quite a bit taller, and the year after it was taller still. For the age of a fir tree can be told by the number of knots on the trunk.

'If only I were as big as the other trees!' sighed the little fir tree. 'Then I should be able to spread my branches really wide, and my tip would look out over the whole forest. The birds would nest in my branches and I should be able to bow and sway gracefully in the wind, like those enormous firs and spruces over there.'

It took no pleasure in the sunshine or birds or the flame-coloured clouds which scudded overhead on fine mornings and evenings.

In winter, when the forest floor was carpeted with a glistening white mantle of snow, a white hare passed by now and then and with one bound would leap right over the top of the tree – oh, how it annoyed the little tree! Two winters passed, and by the third the tree was so big that the hare had to run round it. To grow and grow, taller and taller – that was the only thing that mattered, thought the fir tree.

In autumn the woodmen came and felled some of the bigger trees. This happened year after year, and the young fir tree, which by now had grown quite tall, shuddered when the massive great trees came creaking and crashing to the ground. The branches were lopped off, and the tall trees were barely recognizable as they lay on the ground, thin, stripped and naked. Then they were loaded on to a waggon, and horses dragged them away from the forest.

Where were they going? What lay in store for them?

In the spring when the storks and swallows returned, the tree asked them, 'Do you know where the big trees were taken? Did you by any chance come across them?'

The swallows had no idea, but one of the storks cocked his head on one side as if to consider, and said, 'Yes, I think I know. As I flew across the Mediterranean Sea on my way from Egypt a great many new sailing-ships passed beneath me, their great white sails billowing in the wind. They had enormous masts to hold these sails, and I suspect these were the trees from our forest. They reached up tall, straight and proud towards the sky.'

'How I wish I were big enough to sail on the sea!' sighed the tree. 'What is the sea? What does it look like?'

'Oh, that's much too difficult to explain to you!' replied the stork, making off on his long, thin legs.

'Enjoy your youth!' advised the sunbeams. 'Enjoy your tender green shoots, the fresh young life that is within you.' And the wind kissed the little tree and the dew wept tears over it, but the young tree did not understand.

At Christmas time many quite small trees were felled – some of them not even as big or as old as our fir tree, which was as restless as ever and longed to see the world. These young trees – it was always the prettiest ones – kept their branches. They were loaded on to waggons and carted out of the forest by the horses.

'Where are they going?' asked the fir tree. 'They are no bigger than I. On the contrary, one of them was smaller! Why are they allowed to keep their branches? Where are they being taken?'

'We know! We know!' chirped the sparrows. 'We have often peeped through the windows, down in the city! We know where they are being taken! Oh, they are going to be decorated so splendidly – you cannot imagine! We have often peeped into the windows and seen how each tree is planted in the middle of a warm room and decorated with the most beautiful things – golden apples, honey cakes, toys and hundreds of little lights.'

'And then?' asked the fir tree, all his twigs a-quiver, 'and then? What happens then?'

'We don't know,' replied the sparrows. 'That is all we saw. But they were so beautiful!'

I wonder whether I shall be chosen to be decorated like that! thought the fir tree. What a wonderful life it must be! Far, far better than sailing the salt seas. How I should love to be chosen! If only next Christmas would come quickly! I am just as big and handsome as the trees selected this year. If only they were loading me on to the waggon at this very minute! If only I were already in the warm room, decked out with all that glittering finery! And then? What happens after that? Surely something even better, even more wonderful is bound to happen. Why else would they bother to dress us up so beautifully? There must be some wonderful new experience in store for us! But what? Oh, what a longing fills me! I can hardly wait!

'Enjoy us!' said the fresh air and the sunshine. 'Enjoy your youth here while you can!'

But the fir tree refused to enjoy itself in the sun and fresh air of the forest. It grew and grew. Winter and summer it stood there, decked in the most beautiful green needles, and everyone who saw it exclaimed, 'What a beautiful tree!'

When Christmas drew near again our tree was the very first to be felled. The axe bit deep through the bark into its very centre, and the little tree fell to the ground with a sigh of dismay. What an agonizing pain! There was no thought of joy as it crashed into unconsciousness – only an infinite sadness at being parted from the spot where it had taken root and grown. It knew that it would never again set eyes on the dear old comrades round about or the little bushes and flowers, and perhaps not even the birds.

When the little tree came to itself it was being unloaded in a big courtyard with other young trees, and a man was saying, 'I like that one. Let's have that!'

Two uniformed servants came and bore the little tree into a beautiful big room. There were pictures on the walls, and costly Chinese vases with lions on the lids stood on the ledge beside the great tile stove. There were rocking-chairs, silken sofas, long tables covered with picture books and countless toys of every description.

The fir tree was placed in a large tub filled with sand, but no one could see that it was a tub, for it was hung round with green material and stood on a large, brightly coloured rug. How the little tree quivered in expectation! What would happen next? Men and women came in to decorate it. They hung small packets made of bright, coloured paper from its branches and each packet was filled with sugar candy. Gilded apples and nuts dangled down, as if they were growing from the twigs, and more than a hundred tiny red, white and blue lights were fastened to the tips of the branches. Lifelike dolls, such as the tree had never seen, nestled in the greenery, and at the very top gleamed a great star of golden tinsel. It was magnificent, absolutely magnificent!

'We'll light the candles to-night,' said everyone.

Oh, thought the tree, if only it were evening already! How wonderful it will be when the lights are lit! I wonder what will happen then? Will all the trees of the forest come to see me? Will the sparrows all look through the windows at me? Shall I take root and stand decorated here, winter and summer?

At long last the candles were lit. What brilliance! What splendour! All the tree's branches quivered with excitement, so that one of the candles singed its green needles.

'God protect us!' cried the women, and hastily put out the candle flame.

Now the fir tree dared not quiver again. It was too frightened of losing any of its finery. It was quite dazzled by its own brilliance.

Suddenly the big doors burst open and children poured into the room, as if they were going to upset the tree. A brief moment – but only a moment – they stood and gazed at the tree. Then they yelled for joy and danced round the tree, tearing the little packages from its branches as they danced.

'What are they doing?' wondered the tree. 'What is the meaning of it?' Gradually the candles burnt low and were put out, one after the other. Then the children were allowed to plunder the tree, and they launched themselves on it so roughly that all its twigs snapped and cracked. If it had not been fastened to the ceiling by its gold star it would certainly have been overturned.

The children danced about with their toys, and no one looked at the tree any more, except for the old nanny, who came and peered into the branches, but only to see whether any figs or apples had been forgotten.

'A story! a story!' yelled the children, as they dragged a stout little man up to the tree. 'We will pretend we are in the forest,' he declared, as he sat down under the branches. 'But you can have only one story. Would you like the story of the Three Little Pigs or the story of Humpty Dumpty, who fell off the wall and yet made a name for himself and married the princess?'

'The Three Little Pigs!' cried some of the children. 'Humpty Dumpty' cried others. What a shouting and screaming there was; only the poor fir tree remained silent, thinking, Have I nothing, nothing to do in all

this? But he had already played his part, he had had his turn.

So the man told the story of Humpty Dumpty who fell off the wall and yet made a name for himself and married the princess. And the children clapped and called, 'More! More! Tell us another one!' They wanted to hear about the three little pigs as well.

The fir tree stood quite still and thoughtful. The birds of the forest had never told such a wonderful story! Humpty Dumpty fell off the wall and yet married the princess. Well, well, so that is the way of the world, thought the fir tree, believing that all the man had said must be true. 'Yes, indeed! Who knows? Perhaps I too shall fall off a wall and marry a princess.' And it looked forward immensely to being decorated again with lights and toys, gold and fruit on the following day.

Tomorrow I will not tremble, it thought, I will enjoy my splendour to the full. I shall hear the story of Humpty Dumpty again and perhaps even the story of the Three Little Pigs. All night long the little tree stood quietly, sunk in thought.

Next morning the boys and girls came in again. Ah! thought the fir tree, it's time for my decoration again. But they dragged it from the room and upstairs to the attic and left it standing in a dark corner where the daylight barely managed to penetrate. What is this? thought the tree. What have they brought me here for? How can I hear the story from here? And it leant against the wall and pondered. It had plenty of time to ponder, for there it waited day after day, night after weary night; but no one came. When at last somebody did appear it was only to pile a couple of old boxes in the corner. So now the poor tree stood completely hidden, and it seemed to have been forgotten by the whole world.

Of course, it's the middle of winter outside! thought the tree. They can hardly plant me when the earth is frozen and covered with snow, so they must be keeping me here safe under cover until the spring. How considerate they are! What kind people! But if only it were not quite so dark and lonely! Not even a little hare scampering around! How lovely everything was in the forest in winter, when the snow lay thick on the ground and the hare came hopping past. To think that I wanted to leave the forest! How dreadfully lonely it is here!

'Peep, peep!' said a little mouse, as it scurried out of a hole in the corner. A second mouse followed close behind it. They sniffed at the fir tree and began to climb amongst its branches.

'How frightfully cold it is here!' declared the mice. 'But it's not a bad spot really, is it, you old fir tree?'

'I am not old!' protested the fir tree. 'There are many far older than I!'

'Where have you come from?' they asked. 'And what have you seen?' They were dreadfully inquisitive. 'Tell us all about the most beautiful places in the world. Have you been there? Have you been in the larder, where there is cheese on the shelves and hams hanging from the ceiling? Where you can dance on tallow candles? Where you go in thin and come out fat?'

'No, I have never been there,' replied the fir tree. 'But I know the forest, there the sun shines and the birds sing.' And the tree told the whole story of its life. The little mice had never heard anything like it, and they were most impressed. 'What a lot you have seen!' they exclaimed. 'How lucky you have been!'

'Lucky?' said the fir tree, as he thought over his own story. 'Yes, I suppose I was. I suppose I have had a very happy life.' Then he told them about Christmas Eve, and how he had been decorated with sugar cakes and candles.

'Oh!' piped the mice. 'How lucky you have been, you old fir tree.'

'No, I am not old,' insisted the tree. 'I came from the forest only this winter. I may be very tall, but I am still in my prime.'

'What wonderful stories you tell,' squeaked the little mice. And the following night they returned with a great many other mice, who all wanted to hear about the tree's experiences. And the more he told them, the more clearly he realized how lucky he had been. 'Those were indeed happy days!' he sighed. 'But they will come again, they will come again! Humpty Dumpty fell off the wall and married the princess. Perhaps I shall marry a princess!' And he thought of a dainty little silver birch growing out in the forest – for the fir tree she was a real princess.

'Who is Humpty Dumpty?' asked the mice. So the fir tree related the whole story. He could remember every single word of it. The mice were delighted with it and scampered almost to the top of the tree. The night after, still more mice came along, and on Sunday even two rats. But the rats did not like the story, and that disappointed the little mice, who, truth to tell, had themselves not enjoyed it so much the second time.

'Do you know only the one story?' asked the rats.

'Only the one,' admitted the tree. 'I heard it on my happiest evening, but at the time I did not realize just how lucky I was.'

'Don't you know any stories about cheese and bacon and candle grease?'

'No,' said the tree.

'Well, thanks very much,' said the rats, and scuttled away into their run.

Soon even the mice did not come any more. 'What fun it was,' sighed the fir tree, 'having those lovely little mice gathered round me, listening to my story! But now it is all over. Still, I will think of them and look forward to being taken out of the attic again.'

When did that happen? Well, one morning people came and turned out the attic. The boxes were moved aside and the tree was hauled out. Admittedly it was thrown rather roughly to the floor, but then a servant dragged it to the stairs, where it was bright daylight.

Ah! thought the tree. At last life is to begin again! It

felt the fresh air, the first rays of golden sunshine. ...
Soon it was out in the courtyard. Everything happened
so quickly that the tree forgot to look at itself. There was
so much to see round about. The courtyard led into a
garden full of blossoms. Roses trailed, fresh and scented,
over the little trellis, the lime trees were in bloom and the
swallows swooped about, twittering, but they paid no
attention to the fir tree.

'Now at last I shall live again!' rejoiced the tree, and
spread its branches wide. But, oh, how brown and withered they were! And it lay in a corner amongst weeds and
nettles. The star of golden tinsel was still fastened to the
topmost branch and glinted in the bright sunshine.

In the courtyard were playing a few of the happy
children who had danced so joyfully round the tree at
Christmas. The youngest child ran to the tree and tore
the golden star from the top.

'Look what has been left on that ugly old tree!' he
said, trampling on the branches to make them snap.

As the tree looked at the blossoms and the fresh green
of the garden, it considered its own miserable state and
wished it had been left in its dark corner up in the attic.
It thought of its happy young days in the forest, the
magnificent Christmas evening, and the little mice who
had listened so eagerly to the story of Humpty Dumpty.

'It is all over, all over!' sighed the poor tree. 'If only I
had enjoyed myself when I could. But now it is all
over!'

The gardener came with a big axe and chopped the
tree into little pieces, which he piled up beneath the
boiler. The bright flames flickered, and the tree sighed
deeply, so deeply that each sigh sounded like a shot. The
children heard and left their game to sit watching the
flames and shouting, 'Crack! Bang!'

At each crack, which was a deep sigh, the tree thought of a summer's day in the forest, of a sparkling winter's night when the stars twinkled overhead. It thought of Christmas Eve and of Humpty Dumpty, the only story it had ever heard or could tell ... And then there was nothing left but a heap of ashes.

The children played on in the garden, and the youngest boy had the golden star pinned to his chest – the star that the fir tree had worn on its happiest evening. Now it was all over with the fir tree, and with his story.

All over, all over – that is the way with all stories.

The Invisible Kingdom

In a little farmhouse, which lay perhaps a quarter-of-an-hour's journey from the rest of the village half-way up the mountain, lived a young farmer called George, together with his old father. They possessed so many fields and pastures that neither had a single care. Immediately behind the house began the forest, with oaks and beeches so ancient that the grandchildren of those who had planted them had been dead for over a hundred years. In front of the cottage lay an old broken mill-stone – who knows how it had got there. Whoever sat on it had a magnificent view down into the valley where the river flowed, and to the mountains which rose beyond. Here George would sit and dream for hours on end when his day's work was done, his elbow on his knee and his chin cupped in his hand. And because he did not care for the people of the village and went about his business silent and reserved, as one who broods on many things, the people mockingly called him Dream George.

The older he grew, the more silent he became. When his old father died and had been buried at the foot of a great oak tree, George became completely silent. More than ever now he would sit on the old mill-stone, gazing out over the magnificent valley, watching as the mists of evening crept gradually up the mountains and deepened into darkness until the moon and stars rose in the sky in all their splendour. Then his heart swelled, and the ripples of the river below began to sing, at first very softly, but soon quite clearly. They sang of the mountains from which they came, of the oceans to which they were going, and of the water nymphs who dwelt in the depths of the river. Then the forest would begin to whisper – quite differently from an ordinary forest – and told of the most wonderful things. The old oak tree in particular, which stood over his father's grave, knew a great deal more than all the other trees. The stars stood high in the sky, twinkling and quivering, as if they could hardly resist the temptation to plunge down into the blue of the river or the green of the forest. But the angel standing behind each star held them firmly, saying, 'Stars, stars, let us have no such foolishness. You are far too old for that, many thousands of years and more. Stay where you are and be content.'

It was a wonderful valley! But Dream George was the only one who saw and heard its wonders, for the villagers were dull, ordinary folk and saw only the world around them. From time to time they would fell one of the great old trees in the forest, saw it into pieces and chop up the logs, and when they had built up a good pile they would say, 'Now we can brew ourselves something hot to drink.' And the women would wash their clothes in the river – it was most convenient. And when the stars twinkled in the sky, the villagers would say nothing more than, 'It will be cold tonight. Let's hope our potatoes do not catch the frost!' If George tried to show them something of the magic of their surroundings they would only laugh at him. For they were truly ordinary folk.

One day, as George was sitting on the old, broken mill-stone and thinking how utterly alone he was in the world he fell asleep. He dreamt that a golden swing was hanging from the sky on two silver ropes, and each rope was fastened to a star. On the swing sat a lovely princess, swinging so high that she flew from the sky down to earth and from the earth up to the sky again. Each time the swing came down the princess clapped her hands for joy and tossed him a rose. But suddenly the silver ropes broke and the swing with the princess on it flew into the sky, further and further away, until at last they disappeared from sight. George woke up and looked about him, and there on the old mill-stone lay a great sheaf of roses.

Next day he fell asleep again and dreamt the same dream. And when he woke he found a sheaf of roses lying beside him as before.

So it went on for a whole week, until Dream George began to think his dream must be true if he dreamt it so often. He shut up the house and set off in search of the princess.

After he had journeyed for many days he spied from far off a country where the clouds hung so low that they reached the earth. He marched boldly towards it but soon found himself in a great forest. Suddenly he heard a groaning and whimpering, and as he neared the spot he saw a venerable old gentleman with a silver-grey beard lying on the ground. Two ugly, naked ruffians were kneeling on him and trying to throttle him. George looked round for a weapon with which he could tackle the ruffians, and as he could find nothing he tore a branch from a dead tree. Scarcely had he grasped it than it changed in his hands into a mighty halberd. He fell on the two villains and ran them both through, so that they released the old man with howls of pain and made off into the forest.

George raised the venerable old man to his feet, calmed him and asked why the two naked rogues had wanted to strangle him. The old man explained that he was the King of Dreams and that he had lost his way and wandered by mistake into the kingdom of his greatest enemy, the King of Reality. As soon as the King of Reality knew of his presence, he had ordered two of his serfs to lie in wait for him and kill him.

'What harm have you done the King of Reality?' asked Dream George.

'None whatever,' declared the old man. 'But he is always ready to pick a quarrel, and he hates me more than anyone.'

'But the two men who attacked you were naked!' exclaimed George.

'Yes, indeed,' said the King. 'That is the custom in the Land of Reality – everyone goes naked, stark naked, even the king. They are an abominable people! But you have been kind to me and have saved my life. I should like to prove my gratitude by showing you my country. It is the most magnificent in the world, and my subjects are the dreams.'

The King led the way and George followed. When they came to the place where the clouds reached the earth, the king pointed to a trapdoor, so cunningly hidden in the undergrowth that it would be impossible to find it without knowing where to look. He raised it and led his companion down five hundred steps into a brilliantly lit grotto, which stretched away almost as far as the eye could see. It was indescribably beautiful! There were towering castles built on islands in deep blue lakes, and the islands floated about on the water like ships.

If you wanted to visit one of these castles, all you had to do was to stand on the shore and call:

> 'Come, little castle, come float to me,
> That I may come inside and see.'

Then it would float towards the shore. There were other castles sailing slowly through the sky on clouds. To reach them you would cry:

> 'Come down, my castle in the air,
> That I may come inside and stare.'

Then it would sink gently to the ground.

As well as the castles there were gardens of flowers which filled the air with sweet scent by day, and glowed in the shadows by night, iridescent birds that told stories, and all manner of wonderful things. Dream George was overcome with amazement.

'Now let me show you my loyal subjects, the dreams,' said the King. 'There are three sorts: good dreams for good people, bad dreams for bad people, and dream goblins which I use for my entertainment, for even a king must have his amusements.'

First the King took him into a castle built in such an intricate style as to be quite comic. 'This is where the dream goblins live,' he explained, 'a frolicsome people, fond of playing practical jokes! They do no one any harm, but they delight in teasing.'

'Come here, my little fellow,' he called to one of the goblins, 'and try to be serious for a moment or two.'

Turning to George, the King continued, 'Do you know what this little rascal does when I allow him to go up to the surface of the earth for a brief spell at night? He runs into the nearest house, finds the good householder sound asleep beneath the blankets, hauls him out, carries him up to the top of the church tower, and flings him over. Then he dashes down again before the poor man reaches the ground, catches him in his arms, carries him back home again, and flings him on to the bed with such a thud that the poor fellow wakes up. 'Oh, my goodness!' he declares, as he wipes the sweat from his brow. 'I thought I had fallen from the church tower. Thank goodness it was only a dream!'

'Aha!' exclaims George, 'so you're the rogue who threw me down from the church tower one night! Take care you don't try it again, or it will be the worse for you.'

Next moment another dream goblin bounced out from under the table. He looked rather like a little dog, with a shaggy coat and a long tongue lolling out of his mouth. 'This little fellow is not much better,' said the King. 'He yaps like a dog, yet he has the strength of a giant. When anyone has a nightmare and is terrified, he hangs on to their arms and legs to prevent them running away.'

'Oh, I know him too,' declared George. 'He makes you feel as stiff and rigid as a block of wood as soon as you try to run away. If you try to lift your arm, you can't, and if you try to move your legs, you can't. But I don't think he is always a dog – is he not sometimes a bear or a robber or even worse?'

'I shall never allow any of these dream goblins to visit you again,' the King told George. 'Now let us have a look at the bad dreams. Do not be afraid, they will not

115

harm *you* – they are harmful only to bad people.' They
entered a vast arena surrounded by a high wall, and the
heavy door slammed behind them. The place teemed
with all manner of horrible forms and dreadful mon-
sters. Many seemed to be half man, half beast; many
were completely bestial. George shrank back in terror
against the iron door, but the King again told him to
have no fear. 'Would you not like to see what wicked
people dream?' And he signed to a dream who stood
near by, in the form of a hideous giant carrying a great
mill-wheel under each arm.

'Tell us what you will do tonight,' ordered the King.
The frightful creature pulled his head down below his
shoulders, grinned so that his mouth touched both his

ears, and shook with fiendish glee as he said, 'I will go to a rich man who allowed his father to starve. One day when the old man was squatting on the stone steps of his son's house, begging for a crust of bread, the son came out and said to his servants, "Chase away this cringing old beggar who is making himself such a nuisance!" Now I go to him night after night and crush him between my two mill-wheels until his bones are broken up into tiny pieces. When he is soft and flabby, like a lump of dough, I take him by the scruff of the neck and shake him, saying, "Now let's see you jiggle and dance, you puppet." Then he wakes up, his teeth chattering with terror, and calls to his wife. "Bring me another blanket. I am cold." And when he goes back to sleep, I play the same game all over again. What fun it is!'

Dream George was filled with horror. He tugged the King towards the door, crying, 'I will not stay a moment longer with the bad dreams. It is fearful.' So the King conducted him into a magnificent garden where the paths were of silver, the flower-beds of gold and the flowers of polished jewels. This was where the good dreams were to be found. The first dream he met was a pale young woman with a Noah's ark under one arm and a box of bricks under the other.

'Who is that?' asked George.

'She goes every night to play with a little sick boy whose mother is dead. Poor child, he spends the whole day on his own, for there is no one to look after him. Every evening she goes and plays with him, and she stays the whole night. He always goes to bed very early, and that is why she leaves here before the other dreams, who go much later. Come along, for we must hurry if you are to see them all!'

Deeper and deeper they went into the garden

amongst the good dreams. There were men, women, old folk and children, all with kind and loving faces, and beautifully clad. In their hands they carried all the things the heart could possibly desire. Suddenly George stopped in his tracks and cried out so loudly that all the dreams looked round.

'What is the matter?' asked the King.

'There is my princess who has appeared to me so many times and who brings me roses!' exclaimed George excitedly. 'Oh yes, so it is!' replied the King. 'Didn't I send you a pretty dream? She is probably the prettiest one I have.'

George ran up to the princess, who was sitting swinging on her golden swing. She leapt down the moment she saw him, straight into his arms. He took her gently by the hand and led her to a golden bench, where they sat and told one another how glad they were to have met once more. And when they had finished they began all over again. Meanwhile the King strolled to and fro along the main path through the garden, looking over his shoulder at the clock from time to time, waiting for the princess and George to finish talking. At last he grew impatient and said, 'That's enough now, children! You have a long way to go home, George, and you cannot spend the night here, for I have no beds. You see, the dreams never sleep and they are all away during the night. And you, my princess, it is high time you got ready. Dress all in pink tonight, and then come back to me for your instructions. I must think whom you are to visit tonight and what you are to say to him.'

When he heard that, Dream George felt braver than he had ever felt in his whole life. 'Your Majesty,' he declared, 'I am never going to leave my princess now that I have found her. Either you must let me stay with her here, or you must let her come back to earth with me. I cannot live without her. I love her far too much!' And with these words a huge tear, as big as a hazel nut, welled up in each of his eyes.

'But George, George,' replied the King, 'this is the prettiest dream I have. You cannot take her from me! Yet you did save my life, so let it be. Take your princess and go back to earth. As soon as you reach the surface you must take the silver veil from her face and throw it back to me through the trapdoor. Then your princess will be of real flesh and blood – whereas now she is only a dream!'

Dream George thanked the King from the bottom of his heart and said, 'Dear King, since you have been so very kind to me, I shall dare to ask one more thing of you. I have my princess now, but I have no kingdom, and a princess without a kingdom is quite unthinkable. Could you not let me have one, even if only very tiny?'

'I have no power to create visible kingdoms, George,' said the King with a smile. 'But I can let you have an invisible kingdom, and I promise you it will be as big and as magnificent as I can possibly create.'

'But what is the use of a kingdom if we cannot see it?' asked George.

'You'll soon find out!' answered the King. 'And I assure you it will surpass your wildest hopes. Besides, a real kingdom can sometimes be a most awkward and unpleasant thing. You may wake up one morning to find your prime minister at your beside, saying, "Your Majesty, I need a thousand pounds for state expenses." And when you look in the treasury you may find that you have barely a hundred shillings. What would you do then? Or again, a neighbouring state may declare war on you and conquer you, and the king of the other state will shut you up in a foul dungeon and marry your princess. But this sort of thing can never happen in an invisible kingdom!'

George was still a little downcast, and again said, 'But what is the use of a kingdom if we cannot see it?'

'Oh, you will see it all right,' laughed the King, 'you and your princess. You will see the castles and gardens, the orchards and parklands! You will live in them, walk in them and do what you please in them. But other people will not be able to see any of these things.'

George was overjoyed at this, for he had begun to think that his neighbours might look askance at him if he returned home as a king with his princess. He bade the King a tender farewell and climbed up the five hundred steps with his princess and through the trapdoor; then he took the veil from her face and threw it down to the King. He tried to close the trapdoor, but it was very heavy and fell from his grasp with a crash, and he fell unconscious. When he came to he found himself sitting on the broken mill-stone in front of his cottage with his princess at his side. She was a real princess, of flesh and blood, and she took his hand and gently stroked it, saying, 'Why did you wait so long to tell me how much you loved me? Were you afraid of me?'

The moon rose and shed its silvery beams on the river winding below, the waves lapped against the banks with the tinkling of fairy bells, and the forest rustled and whispered. George and his princess sat and gazed into each other's eyes. Suddenly a dark cloud moved over the moon and something fell from the sky and landed at their feet. The cloud moved away from the moon, and they saw it was a cloth which had been folded many times. They took it up and began to unfold it. But it was very fine and had been folded many hundreds of times, so that it took them a long while. When at last it was completely spread out it looked like an enormous map. A river was marked across the middle of it, with numerous cities, forests and lakes on either side. The map began to grow, and they soon realized that this was the kingdom which their good friend the King of Dreamland had promised them. When they turned to look at their little cottage they found it was a wonderful castle with glass staircases, marble walls and pillars, velvet tapestries and blue towers tapering to fine spires. They rose and walked towards the castle, and as they climbed the steps there was a flourish of trumpets, a roll of drums and a clashing of cymbals. They found all their subjects gathered in the great hall, bowing and curtseying deeply to welcome their king and queen home.

Next morning the news spread like wildfire through the village that Dream George had returned and had brought a wife with him. 'How extraordinary!' the villagers exclaimed, and wondered what sort of a person she was. 'I caught a glimpse of her this morning,' said one farmer, 'as I was coming through the forest. She was standing with him in front of the cottage door. Nothing much to look at, rather small and thin, but good enough for our George. I wonder how they will manage to keep house? He has hardly a penny to his name, and I don't suppose she has either!'

What silly people they were! For they could not see that she was a princess. They were so stupid that they did not even notice that the tiny cottage had turned into a vast castle, for the kingdom really was invisible to foolish people.

George and his queen did not bother themselves about the shallow-minded villagers, but lived happily together in their kingdom. They had six children, and you have never seen such beautiful children, princes and princesses every one. But no one in the village realized it – they were all far too simple.

The Emperor's New Clothes

Many, many years ago there lived an emperor who was inordinately fond of new clothes. He spent all his money on clothes and delighted in showing them off. He took no interest in his soldiers and bothered little about walking amongst his people or going to the theatre, except as opportunities for showing off his new clothes. He had a special tunic for each hour of the day, and whereas in most royal courts you would hear, 'His Majesty is in council,' in this court you would almost invariably hear, 'His Majesty is getting dressed.'

People led a merry life in the great city where he lived, and many strangers visited it. One day two swindlers arrived, posing as weavers and claiming to be able to weave the most beautiful cloth that could possibly be imagined. Not only were the colours and pattern of this cloth quite superb, they said, but any garments made of it possessed the unusual property of being totally invisible to anyone who was unfit for his post or incurably stupid.

What wonderful clothes they must be! thought the Emperor. If I had a suit like that I could soon tell who was stupid and who was intelligent, and which men in my court were unfitted for their posts. Yes, I must have some of this cloth woven for myself without delay! And he gave the two swindlers a generous advance to start work immediately.

They set up a pair of handlooms and pretended to be working at them, but they had no thread on the bobbins. They had the impertinence to insist on the most costly silk and the finest gold thread; but it all went into their own pockets, while they sat and worked at the empty looms until well into the night.

'I should like to know,' said the Emperor, 'how they are getting on with their work.' But to tell the truth he was a little frightened by the thought that a stupid or an incompetent person would not be able to see the material. Not that he was afraid for his own sake, but he felt that someone else ought to see and report to him before he looked for himself. By this time everyone in the whole city knew what wonderful properties the cloth possessed, and they were all curious to find out how stupid and incompetent their neighbours were.

I think I shall send my old Prime Minister to the weavers, thought the Emperor. He is quite reliable, he knows about weaving, he is intelligent, and no one is better suited for his post than he.

So the old Prime Minister went to the room where the two swindlers sat working at their empty looms. 'What on earth!' he exclaimed, and his eyes almost popped out of his head. He saw quite clearly that there was no cloth on the looms, but he was careful not to say so.

The two swindlers told him to come closer, and asked his opinion on the beautiful pattern and brilliant colours, indicating the empty looms with their hands. The poor old Prime Minister stared and stared, but not a thing could he see – for the very good reason that there was nothing there. My goodness! he thought. Am I really so stupid and unfit for my post? I should never have believed it! I must take care that no one finds out! No, I cannot possibly admit that I cannot see the cloth!

'Well, what do you think of it?' asked one of the swindlers.

'Marvellous, quite marvellous!' declared the Prime Minister, looking through his glasses. 'What a wonderful design, and what superb colours! I must run and tell the Emperor. He will be delighted!'

'I'm glad you like it,' said the other swindler, as he proceeded to name the various colours and describe the intricate pattern. The Prime Minister listened with great care to what he was saying, so that he could repeat the description to the Emperor.

The swindlers demanded still more money, more silk and more gold thread for their weaving, and it all found its way into their own pockets. Not a single thread appeared on either of the looms, and yet they sat and worked away at the empty machines.

Soon after this the Emperor sent a second reliable minister to see how things were going and to report to

him how his new clothes were progressing. The same sorry pantomime repeated itself. The minister stared and stared at the empty looms, but not a thing could he see but the bare wooden frames and the air beyond.

'Isn't it a fine piece of material?' asked the two swindlers as they displayed on their arms a length of cloth which was not there.

Surely I cannot be stupid? thought the minister to himself. I suppose I must be unfit for my post. How dreadful! I must take care that no one finds out. Then, turning to the swindlers, he praised the superb colour and design. 'A glorious piece of material!'

By this time the wonderful cloth was almost the sole topic of conversation throughout the city. The Emperor decided that he must see it for himself while it was still on the looms, and went with a select company of his ministers to where the two swindlers were busy working away at the looms with bobbins but no thread.

'Isn't it wonderful?' asked the two ministers who had been there already. 'Do look at these gorgeous colours, and this beautiful design! Have you ever seen anything so splendid?' And they pointed to the empty looms, where they were convinced that everyone else could see more than they could.

This is dreadful! thought the Emperor. I cannot see a thing. Am I stupid, or am I unfit to be emperor? This is really most serious! But these thoughts he kept to himself. 'It is superb,' he said out loud. 'I am quite delighted with it.' And he peered closely at the empty loom frames, for how could he confess that he saw nothing? All his other ministers pressed forward to examine the cloth, and every one of them murmured, 'It is very fine!'

There was to be a great ceremonial parade in a few days' time and everyone advised the Emperor to have his new clothes completed as quickly as possible so that they should be ready in time for the great event. The Emperor was so pleased that he endowed the two swindlers with the title 'Weavers by appointment to the Imperial Court'.

On the eve of the great parade the swindlers sat up all night, apparently hard at work. All the lights were blazing, and anyone who cared to look could easily see that they were working their hardest in order to finish the new clothes in time. They could be seen evidently taking the material from the looms and cutting it with long scissors and sewing it with needles which had no thread. At last they declared that the clothes were ready.

The Emperor came at once with his most distinguished courtiers, and the swindlers held up their arms as if to display the garments. 'See, Your Imperial Highness,' they said. 'Here are the trousers, and here is your jacket, and is this not a superb cloak? Feel for yourself – they are as light as gossamer, you can hardly feel them. But that is the whole joy of them!'

'Yes, indeed,' said the courtiers, but not a thing could they see for there was nothing there to be seen.

'May it please Your Highness to try on these clothes,' said the swindlers. 'We should like to check the fitting in front of this big mirror.'

So the Emperor undressed and the swindlers went through the motions of dressing him, garment by garment, in his new clothes while he turned round and inspected himself in the mirror.

'What a perfect fit!' cried everyone. 'Have you ever seen such a superb costume? Such colours! Such a unique design!'

At this moment the Master of Ceremonies appeared, to announce that the canopy bearers were waiting outside to escort the Emperor to the parade. As he made the announcement the Master of Ceremonies bowed so low that his head almost touched the floor, for he had to conceal the smile that sprang involuntarily to his lips.

'I am ready,' said the Emperor. 'Isn't it a good fit?' Once again he turned in front of the mirror, for he wanted it to appear that he was full of admiration for his wonderful new clothes.

The footmen who were to carry his train fumbled about on the floor with their hands, as if to pick up the train. They walked behind him with outstretched arms as if they were carrying something, for how could they admit that they neither saw nor felt a thing?

So the Emperor stepped out of the palace beneath the magnificent silk canopy, and all the people who were gathered in the streets or clustered at the windows cheered, crying, 'What beautiful new clothes! Have you ever seen such a magnificent train?' For no one would confess that he saw nothing, as that would be admitting that he was either stupid or unsuited for his post. Never before had any of the Emperor's new clothes enjoyed such a tremendous ovation.

'But he has nothing on!' cried a small boy suddenly. 'Shush!' said his father. 'Just listen to the voice of innocence!' But it was too late, for by this time the whisper was spreading through the crowd: 'He has nothing on! He has nothing on!'

This annoyed the Emperor, for he felt that the people were right. But it could not be helped, he would have to brazen it out!

So he stepped out more majestically than ever, followed by his loyal footmen bearing a train which was not there.

The Young King

It was the night before the day fixed for his coronation, and the young King was sitting alone in his beautiful chamber. His courtiers had all taken their leave of him, bowing their heads to the ground, according to the ceremonious usage of the day, and had retired to the Great Hall of the Palace, to receive a few last lessons from the Professor of Etiquette; there being some of them who had still quite natural manners, which in a courtier is, I need hardly say, a very grave offence.

The lad – for he was only a lad, being but sixteen years of age – was not sorry at their departure, and had flung himself back with a deep sigh of relief on the soft cushions of his embroidered couch, lying there, wild-eyed and open-mouthed, like a brown woodland Faun, or some young animal of the forest newly snared by the hunters.

And, indeed, it was the hunters who had found him, coming upon him almost by chance as, bare-limbed and pipe in hand, he was following the flock of the poor goatherd who had brought him up, and whose son he had always fancied himself to be. The child of the old King's only daughter by a secret marriage with an artist – he had been, when but a week old, stolen away from his mother's side, as she slept, and given into the charge of a common peasant and his wife, who were without children of their own, and lived in a remote part of the forest, more than a day's ride from the town.

And it seems that from the very first moment he entered the Court he had shown signs of that strange passion for beauty that was destined to have so great an influence over his life. Those who accompanied him to the suite of rooms set apart for his service, often spoke of the cry of pleasure that broke from his lips when he saw the delicate raiment and rich jewels that had been prepared for him, and of the almost fierce joy with which he flung aside his rough leathern tunic and coarse sheepskin cloak. He missed, indeed, at times the freedom of the forest life, and was always apt to chafe at the tedious Court ceremonies that occupied so much of each day, but the wonderful palace – *Joyeuse,* as they called it – of which he now found himself lord, seemed to him to be a new world fresh-fashioned for his delight.

Upon his journeys of discovery, as he would call them – and, indeed, they were to him real voyages through a marvellous land, he would sometimes be accompanied by the slim, fair-haired Court pages with their floating mantles, and gay fluttering ribands; but more often he would be alone, feeling through a certain quick instinct, which was almost a divination, that the secrets of art are best learned in secret, and that Beauty, like Wisdom, loves the lonely worshipper.

All rare and costly materials had certainly a great fascination for him, and in his eagerness to procure them he had sent away many merchants, some to traffic for amber with the rough fisher-folk of the north seas, some to Egypt to look for that curious green turquoise which is found only in the tombs of kings, and is said to possess magical properties, some to Persia for silken carpets and painted pottery, and others to India to buy gauze and stained ivory, moonstones and bracelets of jade, sandalwood and blue enamel and shawls of fine wool.

But what had occupied him most was the robe he was to wear at his coronation, the robe of tissued gold, and the ruby-studded crown, and the sceptre with its rows and rings of pearls. Indeed, it was of this that he was thinking to-night, as he lay back on his luxurious couch, watching the great pinewood log that was burning itself out on the open hearth. The designs, which were from the hands of the most famous artists of the time, had been submitted to him many months before, and he had given orders that the artificers were to toil night and day to carry them out, and that the whole world was to be searched for jewels that would be worthy of their work. He saw himself in fancy standing at the high altar of the Cathedral in the fair raiment of a King, and a smile played and lingered about his boyish lips, and lit up with a bright lustre his dark woodland eyes.

Outside he could see the huge dome of the Cathedral, looming like a bubble over the shadowy houses, and the weary sentinels pacing up and down on the misty terrace by the river. Far away, in an orchard, a nightingale was singing. A faint perfume of jasmine came through the open window. He brushed his brown curls back from his forehead, and taking up a lute, let his fingers stray across the cords. His heavy eyelids drooped, and a strange languor came over him. Never before had he felt so keenly, or with such exquisite joy, the magic and mystery of beautiful things.

When midnight sounded from the clock-tower he touched a bell, and his pages entered and disrobed him with much ceremony, pouring rose-water over his hands, and strewing flowers on his pillow. A few moments after that they left the room; he fell asleep.

And as he slept he dreamed a dream, and this was his dream. He thought he was standing in a long, low attic, amidst the whir and clatter of many looms. The meagre daylight peered in through the grated windows, and showed him the gaunt figures of the weavers bending over their cases.

The young King went over to one of the weavers, and stood by him and watched him.

And the weaver looked at him angrily and said, 'Why art thou watching me? Art thou a spy set on us by our master?'

'Who is thy master?' asked the young King.

'Our master!' cried the weaver, bitterly. 'He is a man like myself. Indeed, there is but this difference between us – that he wears fine clothes while I go in rags, and that while I am weak from hunger he suffers not a little from overfeeding.'

'The land is free,' said the young King, 'and thou art no man's slave.'

'In war,' answered the weaver, 'the strong make slaves

of the weak, and in peace the rich make slaves of the poor. We must work to live, and they give us such mean wages that we die. We toil for them all day long, and they heap up gold in their coffers, and our children fade away before their time, and the faces of those we love become hard and evil. We tread out the grapes, and another drinks the wine. We sow the corn, and our own board is empty. We have chains, though no eye beholds them; and we are slaves, though men call us free.'

'Is it so with all?' he asked.

'Ay. It is so with all,' answered the weaver. 'But what are these things to thee? Thou art not one of us. Thy face is too happy.' And he turned away scowling, and threw the shuttle across the loom, and the young King saw that it was threaded with a thread of gold.

And a great terror seized upon him, and he said to the weaver, 'What robe is this that thou art weaving?'

'It is the robe for the coronation of the young King,' he answered.

And the young King gave a loud cry and woke, and lo! he was in his own chamber, and through the window he saw the great honey-coloured moon hanging in the dusky air.

And he fell asleep again, and dreamed, and this was his dream. He thought that he was lying on the deck of a huge galley that was being rowed by a hundred slaves. The slaves were naked, but for a ragged loincloth, and each man was chained to his neighbour. The hot sun beat brightly upon them, and the negroes ran up and down the gangway and lashed them with whips of hide. They stretched out their lean arms and pulled the heavy oars through the water. The salt spray flew from the blades.

At last they reached a little bay, and began to take soundings.

As soon as they had cast anchor and hauled down the sail, the negroes went into the hold and brought up a long rope-ladder, heavily weighted with lead. The master of the galley threw it over the side, making the ends fast to two iron stanchions. Then the negroes seized the youngest of the slaves and knocked his gyves off, and filled his nostrils and his ears with wax, and tied a big stone round his waist. He crept wearily down the ladder, and disappeared into the sea. A few bubbles rose where he sank.

After some time the diver rose up out of the water, and clung panting to the ladder with a pearl in his right hand. The negroes seized it from him, and thrust him back.

Again and again he came up, and each time that he did so he brought with him a beautiful pearl. The master of the galley weighed them, and put them into a little bag of green leather.

The young king tried to speak, but his tongue seemed to cleave to the roof of his mouth, and his lips refused to move. The negroes chattered to each other, and began to quarrel over a string of bright beads. Two cranes flew round and round the vessel.

Then the diver came up for the last time, and the pearl that he brought with him was fairer than all the pearls of Ormuz, for it was shaped like the full moon, and whiter than the morning star. But his face was strangely pale, and as he fell upon the deck the blood gushed from his ears and nostrils. He quivered for a little, and then he was still. The negroes shrugged their shoulders, and threw the body overboard.

And the master of the galley laughed, and, reaching

out, he took the pearl, and when he saw it he pressed it to his forehead and bowed. 'It shall be,' he said, 'for the sceptre of the young King.'

And when the young King heard this he gave a great cry and woke, and through the window he saw the long grey fingers of the dawn clutching at the fading stars.

And he fell asleep again, and dreamed, and this was his dream. He thought that he was wandering through a dim wood, hung with strange fruits and with beautiful poisonous flowers. The adders hissed at him as he went by, and the bright parrots flew screaming from branch to branch. Huge tortoises lay asleep upon the hot mud. The trees were full of apes and peacocks.

On and on he went, till he reached the outskirts of the wood, and there he saw an immense multitude of men toiling in the bed of a dried-up river. They swarmed up the crag like ants. They dug deep pits in the ground and went down into them. Some of them cleft the rocks with

great axes; others grabbled in the sand. They tore up the cactus by its roots, and trampled on the scarlet blossoms. They hurried about, calling to each other, and no man was idle.

From the darkness of a cavern Death and Avarice watched them, and Death said, 'I am weary; give me a third of them and let me go.'

But Avarice shook her head. 'They are my servants,' she answered.

And Death said to her, 'What has thou in thy hand?'

'I have three grains of corn,' she answered; 'what is that to thee?'

'Give me one of them,' cried Death, 'to plant in my garden; only one of them, and I will go away.'

'I will not give thee anything,' said Avarice, and she hid her hand in the fold of her raiment.

And Death laughed, and took a cup, and dipped it into a pool of water, and out of the cup rose Ague. She passed through the great multitude, and a third of them lay dead. A cold mist followed her, and the water-snakes ran by her side.

And when Avarice saw that a third of the multitude was dead she beat her breast and wept. She beat her barren bosom, and cried aloud. 'Thou hast slain a third of my servants,' she cried. 'What is my valley to thee, that thou shouldst tarry in it? Get thee gone and come here no more.'

'Nay,' answered Death, 'but till thou hast given me a grain of corn I will not go.'

But Avarice shut her hand, and clenched her teeth. 'I will not give thee anything,' she muttered.

And Death laughed, and took up a black stone, and threw it into the forest, and out of a thicket of wild hemlock came Fever in a robe of flame. She passed through the multitude, and touched them, and each man that she touched died. The grass withered beneath her feet as she walked.

And Avarice shuddered, and put ashes on her head. 'Thou art cruel,' she cried; 'thou art cruel. There is famine in the walled cities of India, and the cisterns of Samarcand have run dry. There is famine in the walled cities of Egypt, and the locusts have come up from the desert. The Nile has not overflowed its banks, and the priests have nursed Isis and Osiris. Get thee gone to those who need thee, and leave me my servants.'

'Nay,' answered Death, 'but till thou hast given me a grain of corn I will not go.'

'I will not give thee anything,' said Avarice.

And Death laughed again, and he whistled through his fingers, and a woman came flying through the air. Plague was written upon her forehead, and a crowd of lean vultures wheeled round her. She covered the valley with her wings, and no man was left alive.

And Avarice fled shrieking through the forest, and Death leaped upon his red horse and galloped away, and his galloping was faster than the wind.

And the young King wept, and said: 'Who were these men, and for what were they seeking?'

'For rubies for a king's crown,' answered one behind him.

And the young King started and, turning round, he saw a man habited as a pilgrim and holding in his hand a mirror of silver.

And he grew pale, and said: 'For what king?'

And the pilgrim answered: 'Look in this mirror and thou shalt see him.'

And he looked in the mirror, and, seeing his own face,

136

he gave a great cry and woke, and the bright sunlight was streaming into the room, and from the trees of the garden and pleasaunce the birds were singing.

And the chamberlain and the high officers of State came in and made obeisance to him, and the pages brought him the robe of tissued gold, and set the crown and sceptre before him.

And the young King looked at them, and they were beautiful. More beautiful were they than aught that he had ever seen. But he remembered his dreams, and he said to his lords: 'Take these things away, for I will not wear them.'

And the courtiers were amazed, and some of them laughed, for they thought that he was jesting.

But he spake sternly to them again, and said: 'Take these things away, and hide them from me. Though it be the day of my coronation, I will not wear them. For on the loom of sorrow, and by the white hands of Pain, has this robe been woven. There is Blood in the heart of the ruby, and Death in the heart of the pearl.' And he told them his three dreams.

And when the courtiers heard them they looked at each other and whispered, saying: 'Surely he is mad; for what is a dream but a dream, and a vision but a vision? They are not real things that one should heed them. And what have we to do with the lives of those who toil for us?'

And the Chamberlain spake to the young King, and said, 'My lord, I pray thee set aside these black thoughts of thine, and put on this fair robe, and set this crown upon thy head. For how shall the people know thou art a king if thou hast not a king's raiment?'

And the young King looked at him. 'Is it so, indeed?'

he questioned. 'Will they not know me for a king if I have not a king's raiment?'

'They will not know thee, my lord,' cried the Chamberlain.

'I had thought that there had been men who were kinglike,' he answered, 'but it may be as thou sayest. And yet I will not wear this robe, nor will I be crowned with this crown, but even as I came to the place so will I go forth from it.'

And he bade them all leave him, save one page whom he kept as his companion, a lad a year younger than himself. Him he kept for his service, and when he had bathed himself in clear water, he opened a great painted chest, and from it he took the leathern tunic and rough sheepskin coat that he had worn when he had watched on the hillside the shaggy goats of the goatherd. These he put on, and in his hand he took his rude shepherd's staff.

And the little page opened his big blue eyes in wonder, and said smiling to him, 'My Lord, I see thy robe and thy sceptre, but where is thy crown?'

138

And the young King plucked a spray of wild briar that was climbing over the balcony, and bent it, and made a circlet of it, and set it on his own head. 'This shall be my crown,' he answered.

And thus attired he passed out of his chamber into the Great Hall, where the nobles were waiting for him.

And the nobles made merry, and some of them cried out to him, 'My lord, the people wait for their king, and thou showest them a beggar,' and others were wroth and said, 'He brings shame upon our State, and is unworthy to be our master.' But he answered them not a word, but passed on, and went down the bright porphyry staircase, and out through the gates of bronze, and mounted upon his horse, and rode towards the Cathedral.

And the people laughed and said, 'It is the king's fool who is riding by,' and they mocked him.

And he drew rein and said, 'Nay, but I am the King.' And he told them of his three dreams.

And a man came out of the crowd and spake bitterly to him, and said, 'Sir, knowest thou not that out of the luxury of the rich cometh the life of the poor? By your pomp we are nurtured, and your vices give us bread. To toil for a master is bitter, but to have no master to toil for is more bitter still. Thinkest thou that the ravens will feed us? And what cure hast thou for these things? Wilt thou say to the buyer, "Thou shalt buy for so much," and to the seller, "Thou shalt sell at this price?" I trow not. Therefore go back to thy Palace and put on thy purple and fine linen. What hast thou to do with us, and what we suffer?'

'Are not the rich and the poor brothers?' asked the young King.

'Ay,' answered the man, 'and the name of the rich brother is Cain.'

And the young King's eyes filled with tears, and he rode on through the murmurs of the people, and the little page grew afraid and left him.

And when he reached the great portal of the Cathedral, the soldiers thrust their halberts out and said, 'What dost thou seek here? None enters by this door but the King.'

And his face flushed with anger, and he said to them, 'I am the King,' and waved their halberts aside and passed in.

And when the old bishop saw him coming in his goatherd's dress, he rose up in wonder from his throne, and went to meet him, and said to him, 'My son, is this a king's apparel? And with what crown shall I crown thee, and what sceptre shall I place in thy hand? Surely this should be to thee a day of joy, and not a day of abasement.'

'Shall Joy wear what Grief has fashioned?' said the young King. And he told him his three dreams.

And when the Bishop had heard them he knit his brows, and said, 'My son, I am an old man, and in the winter of my days, and I know that many evil things are done in the wide world. But canst thou make these things not to be? Wilt thou take the leper for thy bedfellow, and set the beggar at thy board? Shall the lion do thy bidding, and the wild boar obey thee? Is not He who made misery wiser than thou art? Wherefore I praise thee not for this that thou hast done, but I bid thee ride back to the Palace and make thy face glad, and put on the raiment that beseemeth a king, and with the crown of gold I will crown thee, and the sceptre of pearl will I place in thy hand. And as for thy dreams, think no more of them. The burden of this world is too great for one man to bear, and the world's sorrow too heavy for one heart to suffer.'

'Sayest thou that in this house?' said the young King, and he strode past the Bishop and climbed up the steps of the altar, and stood before the image of Christ.

He stood before the image of Christ, and on his right hand and on his left were the marvellous vessels of gold, the chalice with the yellow wine, and the vial with the holy oil. He knelt before the image of Christ, and the great candles burned brightly by the jewelled shrine, and the smoke of the incense curled in thin blue wreaths through the dome. He bowed his head in prayer, and the priests in their stiff copes crept away from the altar.

And suddenly a wild tumult came from the street outside, and in entered the nobles with drawn swords and nodding plumes, and shields of polished steel. 'Where is the dreamer of dreams?' they cried. 'Where is this King, who is apparelled like a beggar – this boy who brings shame upon our State? Surely we will slay him, for he is unworthy to rule over us.'

And the young King bowed his head again, and

prayed, and when he had finished his prayer he rose up, and turning round he looked at them sadly.

And lo! through the painted windows came the sunlight streaming upon him, and the sunbeams wove round him a tissued robe that was fairer than the robe that had been fashioned for his pleasure. The dead staff blossomed, and bare lilies that were whiter than pearls. The dry thorn blossomed, and bare roses that were redder than rubies.

He stood there in the raiment of a king, and the gates of the jewelled shrine flew open, and from the crystal of the many-rayed monstrance shone a marvellous and mystical light. He stood there in a king's raiment, and the Glory of God filled the place, and the saints in their carven niches seemed to move. In the fair raiment of a king he stood before them, and the organ pealed out its music, and the trumpeters blew upon their trumpets, and the singing boys sang.

And the people fell upon their knees in awe, and the nobles sheathed their swords and did homage, and the Bishop's face grew pale and his hands trembled. 'A greater than I hath crowned thee,' he cried, and he knelt before him.

And the young King came down from the high altar, and passed home through the midst of the people. But no man dared look upon his face, for it was like the face of an angel.

The Happy Prince

High above the city, on a tall column, stood the statue of the Happy Prince. He was gilded all over with thin leaves of fine gold, for eyes he had two bright sapphires, and a large red ruby glowed on his sword-hilt.

He was very much admired indeed. 'He is as beautiful as a weathercock,' remarked one of the Town Councillors who wished to gain a reputation for having artistic tastes; 'only not quite so useful,' he added, fearing lest people should think him unpractical, which he really was not.

'Why can't you be like the Happy Prince?' asked a sensible mother of her little boy who was crying for the moon. 'The Happy Prince never dreams of crying for anything.'

'I am glad there is someone in the world who is quite happy,' muttered a disappointed man as he gazed at the wonderful statue.

'He looks just like an angel,' said the Charity Children as they came out of the cathedral in their bright scarlet cloaks and their clean white pinafores.

'How do you know?' said the Mathematical Master, 'you have never seen one.'

'Ah! but we have, in our dreams,' answered the children; and the Mathematical Master frowned and looked very severe, for he did not approve of children dreaming.

One night there flew over the city a little Swallow. His friends had gone away to Egypt six weeks before, but he

had stayed behind, for he was in love with the most beautiful Reed. He had met her early in the spring as he was flying down the river after a big yellow moth, and had been so attracted by her slender waist that he had stopped to talk to her.

'Shall I love you?' said the Swallow, who liked to come to the point at once, and the Reed made him a low bow. So he flew round and round her, touching the water with his wings, and making silver ripples. This was his courtship, and it lasted all through the summer.

'It is a ridiculous attachment,' twittered the other Swallows; 'she has no money, and far too many relations'; and indeed the river was quite full of Reeds. Then, when autumn came they all flew away.

After they had gone he felt lonely, and began to tire of his lady-love. 'She has no conversation,' he said, 'and I am afraid that she is a coquette, for she is always flirting with the wind.' And certainly, whenever the wind blew, the Reed made the most graceful curtseys. 'I admit that she is domestic,' he continued, 'but I love travelling, and my wife, consequently, should love travelling also.'

'Will you come away with me?' he said finally to her, but the Reed shook her head, she was attached to her home.

'You have been trifling with me,' he cried. 'I am off to the Pyramids. Goodbye!' and he flew away.

All day long he flew, and at night-time he arrived at the city. 'Where shall I put up?' he said.

Then he saw the statue on the tall column.

'I will put up there,' he cried, 'it is a fine position, with plenty of fresh air.' So he alighted just between the feet of the Happy Prince.

'I have a golden bedroom,' he said softly to himself as

he looked round, and he prepared to go to sleep; but just as he was putting his head under his wing a large drop of water fell on him. 'What a curious thing!' he cried, 'there is not a single cloud in the sky, the stars are quite clear and bright, and yet it is raining. The climate in the north of Europe is really dreadful. The Reed used to like the rain, but that was merely her selfishness.'

Then another drop fell.

'What is the use of a statue if it cannot keep the rain off?' he said, 'I must look for a good chimney-pot,' and he determined to fly away.

But before he had opened his wings, a third drop fell and he looked up, and saw – Ah! what did he see?

The eyes of the Happy Prince were filled with tears, and tears were running down his golden cheeks. His face was so beautiful in the moonlight that the little Swallow was filled with pity.

'Who are you?' he said.

'I am the Happy Prince.'

'Why are you weeping then?' asked the Swallow; 'you have quite drenched me.'

'When I was alive and had a human heart,' answered the statue, 'I did not know what tears were, for I lived in the Palace of Sans-Souci, where sorrow is not allowed to enter. In the daytime I played with my companions in the garden, and in the evening I led the dance in the Great Hall. Round the garden ran a very lofty wall, but I never cared to ask what lay behind it, everything about me was so beautiful. My courtiers called me the Happy Prince, and happy indeed I was, if pleasure be happiness. So I lived, and so I died. And now that I am dead they have set me up here so high that I can see all the ugliness and all the misery of my city, and though my heart is made of lead yet I cannot choose but weep.'

'What! is he not solid gold?' said the Swallow to himself. He was too polite to make any personal remarks out loud.

'Far away,' continued the statue in a low musical voice, 'far away in a little street there is a poor house. One of the windows is open, and through it I can see a woman seated at a table. Her face is thin and worn, and she has coarse, red hands, all pricked by the needle, for she is a seamstress. She is embroidering passion-flowers on a satin gown for the loveliest of the Queen's maids-of-honour to wear at the next Court-ball. In a bed in the corner of the room her little boy is lying ill. He has a fever, and is asking for oranges. His mother has nothing to give him but river water, so he is crying. Swallow, Swallow, little Swallow, will you not bring her the ruby out of my sword-hilt? My feet are fastened to this pedestal and I cannot move.'

'I am waited for in Egypt,' said the Swallow. 'My friends are flying up and down the Nile, and talking to the large lotus-flowers. Soon they will go to sleep in the tomb of the great King. The King is there himself in his painted coffin. He is wrapped in yellow linen, and embalmed with spices. Round his neck is a chain of pale green jade, and his hands are like withered leaves.'

'Swallow, Swallow, little Swallow,' said the Prince, 'will you not stay with me for one night, and be my messenger? The boy is so thirsty, and the mother so sad.'

'I don't think I like boys,' answered the Swallow. 'Last summer, when I was staying on the river, there were two rude boys, the miller's sons, who were always throwing stones at me. They never hit me, of course; we swallows fly far too well for that, and besides I come of a family famous for its agility; but still, it was a mark of disrespect.'

But the Happy Prince looked so sad that the little Swallow was sorry. 'It is very cold here,' he said; 'but I will stay with you for one night, and be your messenger.'

'Thank you, little Swallow,' said the Prince.

So the Swallow picked out the great ruby from the Prince's sword, and flew away with it in his beak over the roofs of the town.

He passed by the cathedral tower, where the white marble angels were sculptured. He passed by the Palace and heard the sound of dancing. A beautiful girl came out on the balcony with her lover. 'How wonderful the stars are,' he said to her, 'and how wonderful is the power of love!'

'I hope my dress will be ready in time for the State-ball,' she answered; 'I have ordered passion-flowers to be embroidered on it: but the seamstresses are so lazy.'

He passed over the river, and saw the lanterns hanging to the masts of the ships. He passed over the Ghetto, and saw the old Jews bargaining with each other, and weighing out money in copper scales. At last he came to the poor house and looked in. The boy was tossing feverishly on his bed, and the mother had fallen asleep, she was so tired. In he hopped, and laid the great ruby on the table beside the woman's thimble. Then he flew gently round the bed, fanning the boy's forehead with his wings. 'How cool I feel!' said the boy, 'I must be getting better;' and he sank into delicious slumber.

Then the Swallow flew back to the Happy Prince, and told him what he had done. 'It is curious,' he remarked, 'but I feel quite warm now, although it is so cold.'

'That is because you have done a good action,' said the Prince. And the little Swallow began to think, and then he fell asleep. Thinking always made him sleepy.

When day broke he flew down to the river and had a bath. 'What a remarkable phenomenon!' said the Professor of Ornithology as he was passing over the bridge. 'A swallow in winter!' And he wrote a long letter about it to the local newspaper. Everyone quoted it, it was full of so many words that they could not understand.

'Tonight I go to Egypt,' said the Swallow, and he was in high spirts at the prospect. He visited all the public monuments, and sat a long time on top of the church steeple. Wherever he went the Sparrows chirruped, and said to each other, 'What a distinguished stranger!' so he enjoyed himself very much.

When the moon rose he flew back to the Happy Prince. 'Have you any commissions for Egypt?' he cried; 'I am just starting.'

'Swallow, Swallow, little Swallow,' said the Prince, 'will you not stay with me one night longer?'

'I am waited for in Egypt,' answered the Swallow. 'Tomorrow my friends will fly up to the Second Cataract. The river-horse couches there among the bulrushes, and on a great granite house sits the God Memnon. All night long he watches the stars, and when the morning star shines he utters one cry of joy, and then he is silent. At noon the yellow lions come down to the water's edge to drink. They have eyes like green beryls, and their roar is louder than the roar of the cataract.'

'Swallow, Swallow, little Swallow,' said the Prince, 'far away across the city I see a young man in a garret. He is leaning over a desk covered with papers, and in a tumbler by his side there is a bunch of withered violets. His hair is brown and crisp, and his lips are red as a pomegranate, and he has large dreamy eyes. He is trying to finish a play for the Director of the Theatre, but he is too cold to write any more. There is no fire in the grate, and hunger has made him faint.'

'I will wait with you one night longer,' said the Swallow, who really had a good heart. 'Shall I take him another ruby?'

'Alas! I have no ruby now,' said the Prince: 'My eyes are all that I have left. They are made of rare sapphires, which were brought out of India a thousand years ago. Pluck out one of them and take it to him. He will sell it to the jeweller, and buy firewood, and finish his play.'

'Dear Prince,' said the Swallow, 'I cannot do that;' and he began to weep.

'Swallow, Swallow, little Swallow,' said the Prince, 'do as I command you.'

So the Swallow plucked out the Prince's eye, and flew away to the student's garret. It was easy enough to get in, as there was a hole in the roof. Through this he darted, and came into the room. The young man had his head buried in his hands, so he did not hear the flutter of the bird's wings, and when he looked up he found the beautiful sapphire lying on the withered violets.

'I am beginning to be appreciated,' he cried; 'this is from some great admirer. Now I can finish my play,' and he looked quite happy.

The next day the Swallow flew down to the harbour. He sat on the mast of a large vessel and watched the sailors hauling big chests out of the hold with ropes. 'Heave a-hoy!' they shouted as each chest came up. 'I am going to Egypt!' cried the Swallow, but nobody minded, and when the moon rose he flew back to the Happy Prince.

'I am come to bid you goodbye,' he cried.

'Swallow, Swallow, little Swallow,' said the Prince, 'will you not stay with me one night longer?'

'It is winter,' answered the Swallow, 'and the chill snow will soon be here. In Egypt the sun is warm on the green palm-trees, and the crocodiles lie in the mud and look lazily about them. My companions are building a nest in the Temple of Baalbec, and the pink and white doves are watching them, and cooing to each other. Dear Prince, I must leave you, but I will never forget you, and next spring I will bring you back two beautiful jewels in place of those you have given away. The ruby shall be redder than a red rose, and the sapphire shall be as blue as the great sea.'

'In the square below,' said the Happy Prince, 'there stands a little match-girl. She has let her matches fall in the gutter, and they are all spoiled. Her father will beat her if she does not bring home some money, and she is crying. She has no shoes or stockings, and her little head is bare. Pluck out my other eye, and give it to her, and her father will not beat her.'

'I will stay with you one night longer,' said the Swallow, 'but I cannot pluck out your eye. You would be quite blind then.'

'Swallow, Swallow, little Swallow,' said the Prince, 'do as I command you.'

So he plucked out the Prince's other eye, and darted down with it. He swooped past the match-girl, and slipped the jewel into the palm of her hand. 'What a lovely bit of glass!' cried the little girl; and she ran home laughing.

Then the Swallow came back to the Prince, 'You are blind now,' he said, 'so I will stay with you always.'

'No, little Swallow,' said the poor Prince, 'you must go away to Egypt.'

'I will stay with you always,' said the Swallow, and he slept at the Prince's feet.

All the next day he sat on the Prince's shoulder, and told him stories of what he had seen in strange lands. He told him of the red ibises, who stand in long rows on the banks of the Nile, and catch goldfish in their beaks; of the Sphinx, who is as old as the world itself, and lives in the desert, and knows everything; of the merchants, who walk slowly by the side of their camels and carry amber beads in their hands; of the King of the Mountains of the Moon, who is as black as ebony, and worships a large crystal; of the great green snake that sleeps in a palm-tree, and has twenty priests to feed it with honey-cakes; and of the pygmies who sail over a big lake on large flat leaves, and are always at war with the butterflies.

'Dear little Swallow,' said the Prince, 'you tell me of marvellous things, but more marvellous than anything is the suffering of men and of women. There is no Mystery so great as Misery. Fly over my city, little Swallow, and tell me what you see there.'

So the Swallow flew over the great city, and saw the rich making merry in their beautiful houses, while the beggars were sitting at the gates. He flew into dark lanes, and saw the white faces of starving children looking out listlessly at the black streets. Under the archway of a bridge two little boys were lying in one another's arms to try and keep themselves warm. 'How hungry we are!' they said. 'You must not lie here,' shouted the watch-man, and they wandered out into the rain.

Then he flew back and told the Prince what he had seen.

'I am covered with fine gold,' said the Prince, 'you must take it off, leaf by leaf, and give it to my poor; the living always think that gold can make them happy.'

Leaf after leaf of the fine gold the Swallow picked off, till the Happy Prince looked quite dull and grey. Leaf after leaf of the fine gold he brought to the poor, and the children's faces grew rosier, and they laughed and played games in the street. 'We have bread now!' they cried.

Then the snow came, and after the snow came the frost. The streets looked as if they were made of silver, they were so bright and glistening; long icicles like crystal daggers hung down from the eaves of the houses, everybody went about in furs, and the little boys wore scarlet caps and skated on the ice.

The poor little Swallow grew colder and colder, but he would not leave the Prince, he loved him too well. He picked up crumbs outside the baker's door when the baker was not looking, and tried to keep himself warm by flapping his wings.

But at last he knew that he was going to die. He had just enough strength to fly up to the Prince's shoulder once more. 'Goodbye, dear Prince!' he murmured, 'will you let me kiss your hand?'

'I am glad that you are going to Egypt at last, little Swallow,' said the Prince, 'you have stayed too long here; but you must kiss me on the lips, for I love you.'

'It is not to Egypt that I am going,' said the Swallow. 'I am going to the House of Death. Death is the Brother of Sleep, is he not?'

And he kissed the Happy Prince on the lips, and fell down dead at his feet.

At that moment a curious crack sounded inside the statue, as if something had broken. The fact is that the leaden heart had snapped right in two. It certainly was a dreadfully hard frost.

Early next morning the Mayor was walking in the square below in company with the Town Councillors. As they passed the column he looked up at the statue: 'Dear me! how shabby the Happy Prince looks!' he said.

'How shabby, indeed!' cried the Town Councillors, who always agreed with the Mayor; and they went up to look at it.

'The ruby has fallen out of his sword, his eyes are gone, and he is golden no longer,' said the Mayor; 'in fact he is little better than a beggar!'

'Little better than a beggar,' said the Town Councillors.

'And here is actually a dead bird at his feet!' continued the Mayor. 'We must really issue a proclamation that birds are not to be allowed to die here.' And the Town Clerk made a note of the suggestion.

So they pulled down the statue of the Happy Prince. 'As he is no longer beautiful he is no longer useful,' said the Art Professor at the University.

Then they melted the statue in a furnace, and the Mayor held a meeting of the Corporation to decide what was to be done with the metal. 'We must have another statue, of course,' he said, 'and it shall be a statue of myself.'

'Of myself,' said each of the Town Councillors, and they quarrelled. When I last heard of them they were quarrelling still.

'What a strange thing!' said the overseer of the workmen at the foundry. 'This broken lead heart will not melt in the furnace. We must throw it away.' So they threw it on a dust-heap where the dead Swallow was also lying.

'Bring me the two most precious things in the city,' said God to one of His Angels; and the Angel brought Him the leaden heart and the dead bird.

'You have rightly chosen,' said God, 'for in my garden of Paradise this little bird shall sing for evermore, and in my city of gold the Happy Prince shall praise me.'

The Nightingale

In China the Emperor is, of course, Chinese, and all his courtiers are also Chinese. What I am going to tell you happened a very long time ago, but it is well worth relating in case it should be forgotten.

The Emperor's palace at the time of my story was by far the most magnificent in the whole world, full of exquisite porcelain, so delicate that it was almost dangerous to breathe near it. Exotic flowers grew in the garden, and to some of the most beautiful flowers were fastened little silver bells which tinkled merrily in the gentlest breeze, to make sure that no one could pass by without noticing the flowers. The Emperor's garden was beautifully laid out, and stretched so far that not even the gardeners had ever been to the end of it. If you were to walk on and on through the garden you would eventually come to a fine old wood with towering trees and deep lakes. The woodlands rolled right down to the coast where great ships sailed by on the deep blue sea, beneath the spreading boughs of the oldest trees. Among the branches of these trees dwelt a nightingale which sang so sweetly that a fisherman, busy casting his nets on the deep waters, stopped to listen and exclaimed, 'How wonderful! How beautiful!' But then he resumed his work with his nets and forgot all about the nightingale until the following evening when he heard her again, and once more exclaimed, 'How beautiful! How wonderful!'

From every land far and near people came to see and admire the imperial palace and its garden, and they all listened to the nightingale and said, 'That is the best of all!'

When the travellers returned to their own countries they told their compatriots about all they had seen, and scholars wrote countless books about the imperial city, the palace and its extensive garden. But no one omitted to mention the nightingale – on the contrary, the main chapter in the book was invariably devoted to it. Moreover, anyone who could write poetry wrote the most delightful odes to the nightingale in the wood above the deep blue sea.

These books were translated into other languages, and in due course some of them found their way into the Emperor's hands. He sat on his golden throne, reading and nodding his head, for it pleased him to read these glowing descriptions of his empire, his palace and his garden.

'But what is this nightingale they all write about?' exclaimed the Emperor. 'Nightingale? I have never heard of such a creature! What is it? Does such a bird really exist in my empire, and even in my own garden, without my knowledge? To think that I have to learn about it from books!'

He sent for his Chamberlain, who was so aristocratic that he would only reply, 'Pish!' if a lesser mortal addressed him, although 'pish' meant nothing at all.

'Look here!' cried the Emperor, holding up his book. 'According to this book there is a strange and wonderful bird in my land called a nightingale. It is even said to be by far the best thing in my whole empire. How is it that no one has ever told me about it?'

'This is the first I have heard of it!' said the Chamberlain. 'I am sure it has never been presented at court!'

'I insist that it be brought here this very evening,' said the Emperor, 'to sing before me. The whole world seems to know all about it, except me.'

'I have never heard the slightest whisper of such a creature,' declared the Chamberlain. 'However, I will do my best to find it.'

But where was he to look? The Chamberlain ran upstairs and downstairs, hunted through all the rooms and corridors and questioned everyone he met; but no one had heard of a nightingale. So he hastened back to the Emperor and declared, 'Your Majesty, I am sure this nightingale creature must be nothing but a story – a figment of the writer's imagination. You really must not believe everything you see in print, you know! Writers are well known for their powers of invention and imagination!'

'Not at all,' insisted the Emperor. 'This book was sent

to me by the Emperor of Japan, and I refuse to believe that he would send me a pack of lies. I insist on hearing the nightingale! It must be here this evening. I will accept no excuses!'

'What am I to do?' sighed the Chamberlain, as he ran up and down stairs once more, through all the rooms and corridors, followed by half the court, all looking for this wonderful nightingale which the whole world had heard except the court.

At last they discovered a poor little kitchen maid, who said, 'Oh yes, of course I know the nightingale! What a glorious melody she sings! Every evening I am allowed to take the remains of the kitchen supper to my sick old mother, who lives down by the coast. On my way back I often lie down in the woods for a rest, and that is when I hear the nightingale sing. The lovely sound brings tears to my eyes, and it is just as if my mother were kissing me!'

'Little kitchen maid,' said the Chamberlain, 'I will give you a permanent appointment in the imperial kitchen and permission to watch the Emperor himself dine, if you will lead us to the nightingale this very minute, for it is to perform at court this evening, by imperial command.'

So they all went out into the woods where the nightingale was usually to be found. Half the court trailed along. When they had been walking for some time a cow began to bellow in a near-by field.

'Ah!' cried a young nobleman. 'There it is! What a lovely sound, and what power from such a tiny throat! I am sure I have heard it somewhere!'

'That is not the nightingale,' said the little kitchen maid. 'That is only the cattle lowing. We still have a very long way to go.'

Not long afterwards they passed a bog where frogs were croaking.

'Marvellous!' cried the palace priest. 'I hear it now. It sounds just like temple bells!'

'No, no,' said the kitchen maid. 'That is only the frogs. But we have not far to go now – soon we shall hear her.'

Suddenly, through the silence of the forest came the most beautiful song anyone had ever heard. It was the nightingale. 'There she is,' cried the little kitchen maid. 'See – sitting on that bough!' They all looked up and saw a little grey bird on a branch overhead.

'Is it possible?' said the Chamberlain. 'I should never have believed it. Such a plain-looking bird. It must have grown pale at the sight of so many distinguished people!'

'Little nightingale,' called the little kitchen maid, 'our most gracious Emperor would like you to sing for him.'

'With the greatest of pleasure,' replied the bird, and sang an even more haunting melody than before.

'It sounds like crystal bells!' said the Chamberlain. 'And just see how its tiny throat is throbbing!'

'Would the Emperor like me to sing another song for him?' asked the nightingale, who thought that the Emperor was present.

'My most excellent nightingale,' declared the Chamberlain, 'I have the honour to bring you a royal command to attend the palace banquet this evening. You will undoubtedly bewitch His Imperial Highness with your delightful singing.'

'It sounds far better out here in the woods,' said the nightingale, 'but I will gladly come with you to the palace, if that is what the Emperor wants.'

In the palace everything was ready for the banquet.

The walls and floors of porcelain gleamed in the light of a myriad tiny gold lamps. The most beautiful flowers with their silver bells decorated all the corridors. The entire court was assembled, and the little kitchen maid was granted permission to stand at the door of the great hall, for now she had been appointed a full Cook of the Royal Household. Everybody was dressed in his finest clothes, and everyone's eyes were on the little grey bird, to whom the Emperor nodded.

The nightingale sang so beautifully that tears sprang to the Emperor's eyes and ran down his cheeks; she sang again, and everyone present was profoundly moved. The Emperor was so delighted that he commanded a golden slipper to be hung round the nightingale's neck, but all the nightingale wanted was to give pleasure to others. 'I have seen the tears well up in the

Emperor's eyes, and that is enough for me!' she declared. 'To know that I am able to bring an Emperor to
tears is rich enough reward!' And she began to sing again.

'That is a fine way of currying favour!' said the court
ladies who stood round about, and they took a little
water in their mouths and started to gargle when anyone
spoke to them, for they thought their gargling sounded
like the nightingale's song. Even the footmen and
chambermaids showed their approval and that was
praise indeed, for they were always highly critical and
sparing in their praise. Yes, the nightingale was a great
success.

She had to stay on at court and was given a special
cage of her own, with permission to fly outside the
palace twice every day and once every night. She was
accompanied by twelve servants, each of whom held on

to the ribbon fastened round one of her legs, and this was of course most unpleasant.

The whole city talked about the wonderful bird, and whenever two people met, their conversation was sure to turn to the nightingale sooner or later. Eleven children were named after her, although they showed no great promise of being able to sing.

One day the Emperor was handed a large parcel labelled: 'Nightingale'.

'This is sure to be a new book about our famous bird,' he said. But it was not a book – it was an artificial nightingale in a box. It bore a remarkable resemblance to the real nightingale but was studded all over with diamonds, rubies and sapphires. As soon as it was wound up it sang one of the real nightingale's melodies, nodding its head and moving its tail from side to side, and sparkling with silver and gold. Round its neck hung a little label on which was written: 'The nightingale of the Emperor of Japan is but a poor imitation of that of the Emperor of China.'

'It is superb!' they all declared, and the messenger who had brought the clockwork nightingale from Japan was appointed the Chief Imperial Nightingale Bearer.

'Let us have them singing together! We'll have a duet!'

So the two birds had to sing together, but somehow it was not quite right, for the real nightingale sang in her own fashion while the clockwork nightingale sang by means of cylinders. 'It is not the new bird's fault,' said the court musician. 'It keeps perfect time and never misses a beat.' So the clockwork bird had to sing alone, and was greeted with tremendous applause – and the sparkling jewels made it look so much prettier than the live bird.

It sang the same song thirty-three times and showed no signs of fatigue. Most people would willingly have heard it over and over again, but the Emperor thought that the real bird ought to have the chance to display her prowess. But where was she? No one had noticed her slip quietly through the open window and away to her favourite haunt in the green woods.

The Emperor was highly displeased and the courtiers all murmured against the ingratitude of the bird. 'But we still have the better of the two nightingales!' they declared as they wound up the clockwork bird for the thirty-fourth time. The court musician was unstinting in his praise of the artificial bird, and assured everyone that it was much better than the real one, not only because of the sapphires and glittering diamonds, but also because of the quality of its voice. 'You see, my lords and ladies,' he said, 'you can never be quite sure what sort of a song the real nightingale will produce, but you know exactly what and how the clockwork bird will sing. Its singing does not vary in the slightest from one performance to the next. It has all been carefully calculated in advance and it can be demonstrated exactly which note will fall where, and what time will be allocated to each note. There can be no possible variation!'

'Yes, yes, of course!' they all declared. 'We agree with you entirely!' And the court musician was instructed to take the clockwork nightingale to show to the people on the following Sunday. 'They must hear it sing too,' commanded the Emperor. So the people saw and listened, and were quite delighted with the bird. Some said, 'Oh!' and others said, 'Ah!' as they nodded their heads and held up one finger, in typical Chinese fashion. But the poor fisherman who had heard the real nightingale sing, said to himself: 'Well, I suppose it is quite pleasant; it does bear a faint resemblance to the real thing, but there is something lacking – I'm not quite sure what!'

The real nightingale was banned from the empire, while the clockwork one was given a silken cushion at the Emperor's bedside. It had been given a great many gifts of precious stones, and these lay scattered around it, while it enjoyed the official title of Imperial After-Dinner Singer, with the rank of first-class courtier of the left-hand side (for you will appreciate that the Emperor gave special preference to the side his heart was on, and most emperors have the heart on the left-hand side). The court musician wrote twenty-five tomes on the clockwork bird, and this work of scholarship was so learned and contained so many impossibly difficult Chinese words, that all the people said they had read it and understood it. Otherwise, of course, they would have been considered very stupid.

So a whole year went by. The Emperor, the court and countless other Chinese knew every single note in the bird's repertoire off by heart, and this pleased them no end for it meant that they could join in. Even the street urchins sang nightingale songs, and so did the Emperor. It was all quite delightful.

One evening, however, when the artificial bird was singing at its very best and the Emperor lay in bed listening, there was a sudden whirring of wheels and clicking of springs, and then – silence!

The Emperor leapt from his bed and sent for the court physician, but what could he do? They sent for the watchmaker, who managed – after a great deal of prying into the bird's inside – to put things right, but he said that it could be played only very sparingly, for all the gears were worn out and it was quite impossible to make new ones which would be at all reliable. What lamentation there was at the palace! Only once a year were they allowed to hear the nightingale, and even that was risky, although the court musician gave a public speech in which he assured everyone that the nightingale was as good as ever.

Five years elapsed, and suddenly the whole land was plunged in deep sorrow, for their Emperor, who had governed their lives for so long, suddenly fell ill and was said to be on his death-bed. A new Emperor was even elected in advance, while the common people crowded round the palace gates to ask the Chamberlain for news of the Emperor.

'Pish!' replied the Chamberlain, with a shake of his head.

Cold and pale, the Emperor lay in his magnificent great bed. The whole court considered him as good as dead, and everyone ran to the new Emperor's service. The footmen ran outside to chatter about it, and the maids all held a coffee party to discuss the new Emperor. In all the rooms and corridors the floors were covered with felt so that not a sound should be heard, and a ghostly silence pervaded the royal apartments. But the Emperor was not dead yet. Still and pale, he lay in his magnificent bed, looking up at the heavy velvet hangings with their huge gold tassels, and beyond them to the open window, through which the moon shone down.

The poor Emperor could hardly breathe. He felt as if a great weight pressed him down. He forced his weary eyes open and saw that it was Death sitting on his chest. He was wearing the imperial crown on his head and held the Emperor's golden sabre in one hand and the royal flag in the other. From the folds of the velvet hangings strange faces peeped forth, some of them ugly, others gentle and pitying. They were the Emperor's bad and good deeds looking down on him now that Death had him in his clutches.

'I did not know it would be like this,' sighed the Emperor. 'Music!' he called. 'Bring me the great Chinese drum to drown the incessant chatter of these dreadful creatures!' But their voices could still be heard, and Death sat nodding like a mandarin.

'Music, music!' cried the Emperor again. 'My little golden nightingale, sing to me! I gave you gold and jewels, I even hung my golden slipper round your neck, why do you not sing?'

But not a sound came from the bird, for there was no one to wind her up. Death continued to gaze down at him with sightless eyes. A dreadful silence hung over the room.

Suddenly, just outside the window, a wonderful singing burst forth. It came from the little living nightingale, perched outside on a branch. She had heard of the Emperor's desperate need and had come to sing comfort and hope to him. The sweet melody rose and fell and the ghostly faces grew paler and paler as the singing filled the quiet night air. Faster and faster pulsed the blood through the Emperor's weak body, and even Death looked up and called, 'Sing on, sweet bird, sing on!'

'Gladly,' replied the nightingale, 'if you will give me the Emperor's golden crown and sabre, and his flag.'

So Death gave up each prize in exchange for a song, and the little nightingale sang of the quiet graveyard where the white roses bloom and the fragrance of lilac blossom fills the air, and the green grass is moistened by the tears of the mourners. Death felt a great longing for his own garden, and sailed away through the open window like a cold white mist.

'Thank you!' said the Emperor. 'Thank you a thousand times, you heavenly bird! I banished you from my kingdom and you have come and chased away the evil spirits from my bed, and have driven Death himself from my heart! How can I ever reward you?'

'You have rewarded me already,' said the nightingale. 'Did I not tell you, when first I sang to you, that tears in the listener's eyes are the finest possible reward for any singer? But you must sleep now, sleep and grow well and strong again! Come, I will sing you to sleep.'

And she sang – and the Emperor fell into a deep, blissful sleep.

When he awoke, the sun's rays were streaming through the window on to his bed, and he felt restored to health and strength. Not one of his servants came, for they all thought that he was dead; but the nightingale was still singing.

'Stay near me for ever!' said the Emperor. 'Sing whenever you feel like it, and I will have the clockwork bird smashed into a thousand pieces.'

'No, do not do that,' said the nightingale. 'It did what it was made to do – it could hardly do more! I cannot live in your palace, but let me come here whenever I feel like it. I promise to sit on this branch in the evenings and sing to you, and fill your heart with pleasant thoughts. I will sing to you of joys and sorrows, of good and evil, and of things which are concealed from you. I see much that you cannot see as I fly over the fisherman's boat, the labourer's cottage, over those who are far from you and your court. Your heart means more to me than your crown, so I will sing for you. But you must promise me one thing.'

'Anything you want!' declared the Emperor, as he stood arrayed in his imperial regalia, and he laid his heavy golden sabre to his heart.

'One thing only I beg of you. Do not tell a soul that you have a little bird who tells you everything, and then all will go well.' And with these words the nightingale flew away.

The servants came in to fetch their dead master. Yes, there they stood, amazed, and the Emperor said, 'Good morning!'

The Snow Queen

A Fairy-tale in Seven Stories

First Story

THE MIRROR AND ITS FRAGMENTS

Well, let's begin. When our story is over, we shall be wiser than we are now.

There was once a wicked goblin, the very worst of all, for he was the Devil himself. One day he was particularly pleased with himself, for he had just made a magic mirror which had the peculiar property of shrinking up everything good and beautiful that was reflected in it, and magnifying everything wicked and ugly out of all proportion. In this mirror the most beautiful views looked like mashed spinach, and even the best people looked repulsive in it or appeared to stand on their heads, with features distorted beyond all recognition. If a good man had a single freckle, the mirror would make it seem to spread all over his nose and mouth. And the Devil found this highly entertaining. If a man had a kind, generous thought, the mirror would show a ghastly leer on his face.

All his pupils, whom he instructed in the School for

Goblins, spread abroad the news of the wonderful mirror, and declared that it showed the true face of the world and human kind. They carried the mirror all over the world, with the result that there was soon not a man alive who had not been sadly misrepresented in it.

Then they thought it would be fun to take it up to heaven and amuse themselves at the expense of God and his angels. The higher they flew with it, the more the mirror seemed to grin back at them till they found great difficulty in holding it fast.

Higher and higher they flew, nearer and nearer to God and his angels. At length the mirror quivered and shook so violently in its grimaces that it slipped from their grasp, and fell to earth, where it smashed into millions and millions of pieces.

In this way it caused more harm and suffering than ever before, for many of the splinters, hardly as big as a grain of sand, flew about in the air until they landed in somebody's eye. They made people see everything as distorted or, even worse, gave them eyes only for what was evil or ugly, for each splinter possessed the same evil properties as the mirror itself. But the worst damage of all occurred when someone caught a splinter in his heart, for then his heart became cold and froze to a lump of ice. Some fragments of the mirror were so big that they were used for window-panes, but it was a great misfortune to look into friends' houses through panes such as these. Some fragments were made into spectacles, and anyone putting them on saw everything distorted and was quite unable to tell right from wrong.

The Devil laughed till his stomach wobbled, so amused was he. There are still tiny splinters of glass drifting about in the air, and we shall hear more of these.

A LITTLE BOY AND A LITTLE GIRL

In the big city, where there are so many houses and
people that there is no room to spare for gardens and
most people have to be satisfied with a few flowerpots,
lived two poor children who none the less had a garden
just a little bigger than a flowerpot. They were not
brother and sister, but they were extremely fond of each
other. Their parents lived in attic rooms which were
right next door to one another. At the point where the
roofs joined and the gutter ran between there was a little
window in each attic. All the children needed to do to go
from one window to the other was to step over the gutter.
In front of each window there was a large wooden box
where the herbs that were needed for cooking were
grown, and a little rose-bush besides, one in each box,
which flourished and grew. Then it occurred to the
parents that it would be a good idea to place the window-
boxes across the gutter so that they reached almost from
one window to the other and looked as though they were
two flowerbeds. Pea runners from the two boxes inter-
twined, and the rose-bushes joined overhead to form an
arch of leaves and blossoms. From time to time the
children were allowed to take their little chairs out on to
the window-boxes, and they would sit beneath the roses
and play together.

Winter, of course, put an end to this kind of fun; for
the windows were often stuck fast with thick ice. Then
the children would warm pennies on the stove and press
them against the window-panes to melt a little peep-
hole. How perfectly round these holes were! What fun
it was to peep through and see another laughing eye

looking back from a peep-hole in the opposite window!

The little boy was called Kay and the little girl Gerda. Outside swirled the snowflakes. 'There are the white bees swarming,' said Kay's grandmother.

'Do they have a queen bee, as ordinary bees do?' the boy asked.

'Yes, indeed,' replied his grandmother. 'She flies where the snowflakes swirl thickest. She is the largest of them all and never settles on the ground for long, but sweeps upward again to the black snow-clouds. On many a winter night she flies through the city streets, peering through the windows, which then adorn themselves with ice-flowers.'

'Oh yes, I have seen them!' cried the children, and now they knew that it was quite true.

'Can the Snow Queen come inside?' asked Gerda. 'Just let her come!' said Kay. 'I would put her on the stove and watch her melt.' But his grandmother stroked his hair and told him other stories.

That evening before going to bed, when little Kay was already half undressed, he climbed up on the chair by the window and peeped through the little peep-hole. Outside, snowflakes were falling, and one of them, the biggest, settled on the edge of the window-box. The snowflake grew bigger and bigger, until at last it turned into a beautiful woman. Her gown was of the finest white cambric and was scattered with millions of glistening, star-shaped snowflakes. She was dainty and slender, but made of ice, of pure, shimmering ice, and yet she was alive. Her eyes flashed like two bright stars, but there was neither peace nor repose in them. She nodded towards the window and waved her hand to him. The boy was frightened and jumped down from his

chair. And then it seemed as if a great white bird flew past the window outside.

The following day the frost was severe, but soon afterwards it began to thaw, and spring followed shortly after that. The sun shone, the grass sprouted, the swallows built their nests, and once again the children sat together in their little garden high above the street.

That summer the roses were more beautiful than ever. Little Gerda had learnt a song about roses which reminded her of her own. She sang the song to her little playmate, and he joined in. And the children held hands, kissed the roses and looked up into the glorious sunshine. What wonderful summer days those were! How delightful it was to sit up there so high above the street, beneath the fresh rose-bushes, which seemed as if they would go on blossoming for ever!

One day Kay and Gerda were sitting reading a book together – the clock in the great church tower had just struck five – when suddenly Kay cried out in pain. 'Oh, something has stabbed my heart! And I have something in my eye, too!'

Little Gerda flung her arms round his neck; he blinked his eyes but, no, there was nothing to be seen.

'Oh, it's all right now,' he said. But it was by no means all right. It was one of the glass splinters from the goblin's mirror – do you remember it? – the mirror that distorted everything good and beautiful, and magnified everything nasty and ugly? A sharp splinter had penetrated right into poor Kay's heart. It was no longer painful, but it was still there and it would turn his heart to ice.

'Why are you crying?' he asked. 'Crying makes you look ugly! I can't stand it. Ugh!' he exclaimed all at once. 'That rose has been eaten by worms. And that one is all crooked. How ugly all these roses are, and so is this whole window garden.' And with these words he kicked the boxes to pieces and tore down both the roses.

'Kay, what are you doing?' cried Gerda. And when he saw how horrified she was, he pulled off another rose, leapt through his own window and left poor Gerda outside on her own.

From now on, whenever she came to him with her picture-book, he would say it was fit only for babies. If her grandmother tried to tell them stories, he would scoff at them. He would even stand behind the old woman, with her glasses on his nose, and mimic her to make people laugh. Before long he could imitate perfectly the voice and mannerisms of everyone in the street, and people used to say, 'What a strange lad he is!' But it was only the glass splinters in his heart and eye that made him as he now was. For the same reason he would torment and tease little Gerda, who had never done him any harm. Even his games changed and became more serious than they had been before.

One winter's day when the snowflakes were falling, he poked a corner of his dark blue jacket out of the window to collect some snow-flakes and held a magnifying glass in his other hand.

'Look through the glass, Gerda,' he said, and he showed her how each snowflake was a perfect, ten-pointed star of dazzling beauty.

'See how perfect they are!' he exclaimed. 'How much lovelier they are than real flowers! If only they would not melt!'

Not long after this Kay came with his big gloves on his hands and his sledge on his back and yelled to Gerda, 'I'm off to play in the square with the other boys.'

One of the great games for the boldest boys in the square was to tie their sledges to the horse-drawn sleighs belonging to farmers from the outlying districts, and to go part of the way with them. What fun it was! While they were busy playing, a great white sleigh came gliding by, and in it rode a figure wrapped in a rough white fur, and wearing a white fur hat. The sleigh wheeled twice round the square, and the second time round Kay quickly fastened his sledge behind it and allowed himself to be pulled after it. Faster they went, faster and faster, from one white street to the next, and the white-shrouded form in front turned and waved to Kay, just as if they were old acquaintances. Every time Kay tried to loosen the rope the figure waved to him again, and he stayed where he was. On they sped through the city gates.

Now the snow fell thicker and faster than ever and Kay could hardly see his hand in front of his eyes. Faster and faster they flew, with the wind howling like a thousand demons in his ears. He called for help, but his cries were drowned in the frantic swirl of the snow. By this time the sledge seemed to be almost airborne and he could see ditches and dykes whipping past beneath him. Sheer terror held Kay in its grip and he tried to pray, but all he could say was his multiplication tables!

The snowflakes became bigger and bigger until at last they looked like great white hens. Suddenly the storm died down as quickly as it had begun, the sleigh came slowly to a halt and Kay saw the figure in front stand up. Hat and cloak were pure snowy white. It was a woman – tall, slim and dazzling white. It was the Snow Queen.

'We have made good time,' she said. 'But you are shivering with cold – come in under my bearskin cloak!' And she lifted him gently into her sleigh and wrapped him inside her cloak. He felt as if he were sinking into a snow drift!

'Are you still cold?' she asked as she kissed him. Her kiss was colder than ice and it seemed to pierce his heart, even though that was a lump of ice. He felt sure he was going to die – but only for a moment, for gradually he became less conscious of the intense cold.

'My sledge! Where is my sledge!' he cried, so the Snow Queen tied it to one of her great hens which flew behind the sleigh. She kissed Kay again, and this time he forgot all about Gerda and Granny and everything at home.

'I must not kiss you any more,' she said, 'or I shall kiss you to death!'

Kay looked up at her. She was indescribably beautiful. It would have been hard to imagine more lovely and more intelligent features. No longer did she look as if she were made of ice, as she had done that time when she had sat outside his window and waved to him. No longer was he afraid of her. He chattered away happily, telling her how good he was at mental arithmetic, even fractions, how he knew the geography of the country and what the population was. How amused she was by his childish prattle! As she smiled at him, it struck him that perhaps he did not know very much after all.

High in the air they flew through the great black snow-clouds, while the storm whistled and raged about them and strange, haunting melodies filled the air. Over land and sea they flew, while down below them the

bitter, cold wind blustered and the wolves howled. Now and then a huge raven would appear through the swirling snow and screech at them, only to disappear into the storm as suddenly as it had come. When darkness fell the storm abated and the silvery moon shone clear and bright in the sky. All through the next day Kay slept soundly at the Snow Queen's feet.

Third Story
THE FLOWER GARDEN OF THE
ENCHANTRESS

Meanwhile what did little Gerda do when Kay failed to return? She made desperate attempts to trace him, but all that the other boys could tell her was that he had tied his sledge to the back of a magnificent white sleigh and had been carried at a tremendous speed along the street and out of the city gates. No one had the remotest idea what had happened to him after that, and little Gerda wept bitter tears. Most people were convinced that he must have been drowned in the river, but Gerda did not give up hope so easily.

What desperately long winter months those were! At last the first spring days came with their welcome blessing of warm sunshine.

'I suppose Kay must be dead!' sighed Gerda.

'Don't you believe it!' murmured a sunbeam.

'Surely he is dead?' she repeated, turning to the little swallows.

'What makes you so sure?' they replied. And at last Gerda's own hopes revived.

'I shall put on my beautiful new red shoes,' she said one morning, 'for Kay has never seen them. I must go and ask the river if it knows what happened to him.'

The first flush of dawn still glowed in the eastern sky as she gently kissed her sleeping grandmother, slipped on her new red shoes and went out through the city gates towards the river.

'Is it true that you took my little friend away from me?' she asked the river. 'I will give you my beautiful new red shoes if you will bring him back to me.'

It seemed as if the water swirled ever so slightly towards her, so she took off her red shoes, her most valuable possessions, and flung them into the river. But she had not thrown them very far and the water soon washed them up on the bank, as if to say that it knew nothing of Kay and would not deprive her of such lovely shoes. But Gerda was persistent. She climbed into a little boat which lay moored in the reeds in order to throw the shoes further out into the river. But the boat was not firmly tied and drifted quickly out into the current, and before she realized what was happening Gerda found herself being swept away downstream. She was terrified and began to call for help, but no one heard her cries. Her little red shoes bobbed merrily along behind her, but they could not catch up with the boat.

How beautiful was the countryside through which she passed! Spring flowers and blossoming almond trees lined the banks, while sheep and cows grazed on the gentle green slopes beyond.

Gerda took courage from the hope that perhaps the river had accepted her gift after all and was taking her to Kay. After some time she came to a great garden full of flowers and cherry trees, in the midst of which stood a pretty little house with curious red and blue windows and a thatched roof. By the door stood two little wooden soldiers, who presented arms as she drew near. She called to them, for at first she thought they were real people, but not unnaturally they made no reply.

The river carried the boat quite close to the bank, and Gerda called again for help. This time a wrinkled old woman came out of the house, leaning on a crutch and wearing an immense straw hat whose brim was painted with all sorts of flowers.

'My poor child!' cried the old woman. 'What in the world are you doing on such a dangerous river?' She waded into the swirling waters and caught the boat with her crutch, brought it to the bank and helped Gerda to step out on to dry land.

Gerda was delighted to feel firm ground beneath her feet, but she was a little afraid of the old woman, who said, 'Come now, and tell me who you are and where you have come from.'

So Gerda told her the whole story and asked if by any chance the old woman had seen Kay. She replied that she had seen no sign of him yet, but that doubtless he would turn up. Meantime, Gerda was to stay with her, and pick the flowers and eat the cherries when they were ripe. Were her flowers not much more beautiful than the ones in Gerda's picture-book? She took Gerda by the hand and led her into the house and closed the door.

'For years I have longed for a little girl like you,' said the old woman. 'I am sure we shall get on splendidly together.' She began to comb Gerda's hair, and as she combed so Gerda forgot about her home and little Kay, for the old woman was an enchantress. But she was not a wicked witch, and there was no evil in her magic. She worked spells only for her own amusement, and she wanted so much to keep little Gerda with her. When Gerda was not looking, she went out into the garden and touched all the roses with her crutch, and immediately they sank down into the black earth, no matter how exquisite their blooms. Not a trace was left of them, for the old woman feared that the sight of roses might remind Gerda of her own and make her think of Kay.

Then she took Gerda into the flower garden. How lovely, how colourful it was! Flowers of every season blossomed side by side in glorious profusion. Gerda danced for joy and played beneath the cherry trees until sunset. Then she was given a fine bed with red silk cushions filled with sweet-smelling violets, where she slept soundly and dreamt as sweetly as a princess on the eve of her wedding.

Next day she played in the sunshine amongst the flowers, and so it went on day after day. Soon Gerda knew every flower in the garden, but although there were so many different kinds she could not help feeling that there was one missing. One day her glance fell on the old woman's straw hat with the flowers painted round the brim, and the most beautiful of all was a rose! For the old woman had forgotten to remove it from her hat.

'What!' exclaimed Gerda. 'Are there no roses here?' And she ran all over the garden, searching and searching, but not a rose could she find. She flung herself on the ground and sobbed her heart out, and her tears fell on the very spot where a rose-bush had sunk into the ground. As soon as her warm tears touched the earth the rose shot up as beautiful as ever, laden with blooms. Gerda threw her arms round it and kissed each bloom in turn, and she remembered her roses at home and her little friend Kay.

'How I have frittered away my time!' she exclaimed. 'I should have been searching for Kay! Do you know where he is?' she asked the roses. 'Is he dead?'

'He is not dead,' they replied. 'We have been under the ground for a long time, where all the dead dwell, and there was no sign of Kay.'

'Thank you,' said Gerda, and went to the other flowers, peeped into them and asked, 'Don't you know where little Kay is?'

All the flowers stood drinking in the golden sunshine and dreaming their own dreams, but none of them knew anything of Kay.

The fire lily told a story of India, but this was of no interest to Gerda. She turned to the pale blue windflower, and what story did he have to tell her?

'By following a narrow path, you come to an ancient castle. The old red walls are covered with thick creepers right up to the balcony, and there stands a beautiful girl. She leans over the balustrade, gazing down to the path.

No rose upon its stem is as fair as she, no apple blossom is as gentle as she, as it is borne on the breeze that rustles her silken gown. Isn't he coming yet?'

'Do you mean Kay?' asked Gerda.

'I am telling my story, my dream,' replied the windflower.

And what did the snowdrop have to say?

'A swing hangs from a tree on long, long ropes, and two little girls are swinging on it, their snow-white dresses fluttering in the breeze, the long green ribbons streaming from their hats. Between them stands their little brother. In one hand he is holding a bowl of soapy water, and in the other he holds a clay pipe. He is blowing bubbles, lovely bright bubbles which hover in the air all around them. A new bubble is even now quivering on the pipe, eager to be set free. A little black dog hops on its hind legs, wanting to swing too. The swing goes up, the little dog falls and barks, the bubble bursts. That is my dream – a swing and a bursting bubble.'

What about the hyacinths?

'There are three beautiful sisters, fair and gentle. One of them is dressed in red, the second in blue and the third in white. Hand in hand they are dancing in silvery moonlight on the banks of a calm lake. They are real girls – not fairies. The air is filled with a sweet perfume which becomes stronger and stronger. The girls lie down in three coffins which are borne away over the still waters of the lake. Fireflies hover like tiny lights. Are the girls dead? The perfume of flowers seems to say that they are. The church bells are tolling.'

'You make me sad,' said Gerda. 'Why should the girls be dead? Is Kay dead? The roses have been under the ground and they assure me he is not there.'

'Kling, klang,' rang the hyacinth bells. 'We are not

ringing for Kay. We do not know him. We are telling
our own story – the only one we know.'

So Gerda went to the buttercup, whose bright yellow
petals peeped through the long grass.

'You look just like a little sun shining there,' she said.
'Can you tell me where I can find my friend?'

The buttercup smiled sweetly at her. What sort of a
story would it have to tell?

'I see God's golden sun shining into a little courtyard
on a fine spring morning, lighting up the old stone walls
and the cobbles. An old grandmother is sitting in a rock-
ing-chair, enjoying the sun's warm rays. The sun tip-
toes lightly over the cobbles and kisses the old lady, and
its kiss is golden – the pure gold of love and kindness and
joy. Isn't that a good story?' said the buttercup.

'Oh, my poor old grandmother!' sighed Gerda. 'I am

sure she must be worrying about me. But I shall soon be home, bringing Kay with me. What is the use of asking all these flowers for news of Kay when each of them knows only its own story?'

She tucked up her skirt in order to run faster, but a daffodil brushed against her knees as she was leaping over it, and whispered, 'Do you know what?' So Gerda bent down to listen, and this is what she heard.

'I can see me,' said the daffodil. 'I can see myself! Oh, how lovely I am! Up in the attic I see a dancer skipping about half dressed, now on one leg, now on the other. She seems to be treading the whole world under foot. Now she is pouring water out of a teapot on to her bodice. Cleanliness is a beautiful thing. Her little white dress is hanging on a peg. She takes it down and pours water on it from the teapot, and hangs it up to dry. Now she is putting it on and is tying a saffron yellow scarf round her neck, making the dress look even whiter. Slowly she stretches one leg up, raising it high. See! She is like a flower on a stalk! I can see myself! I can see myself!'

'Why are you telling me all this?' asked Gerda impatiently. 'None of this concerns me.' And she hurried out of the garden.

The gate was locked, but the catch was almost eaten away by rust and broke as soon as she twisted it. Gerda took a quick look over her shoulder to see if she was being followed, and fled from the garden in her little bare feet. She ran and ran until she was out of breath, and then she sat down to rest on a boulder. As she looked about her she saw that summer had passed and it was now autumn, for all the seasons in the enchanted garden were mixed up together and she had no idea how long she had been there. 'How long I must have stayed!' she exclaimed. 'It is autumn already and I have no time to lose.' And she rose and hurried on her way.

The weather grew colder, and her little feet were sorely cut and bruised on the rough, stony ground. The long willow leaves turned yellow and fluttered down one by one. Only the sloe still bore fruit. The whole world seemed grey and desolate.

Fourth Story
PRINCE AND PRINCESS

Weary and footsore, Gerda had to rest again. A great black crow came hopping through the snow and paused to observe her, cocking his head inquisitively from side to side and peering at her out of the corner of his eye.

'Caw! Caw! Good morning to you!' said the crow. He sat and watched her for a few minutes, and then asked her why she had come out all alone into the great wide world. So Gerda told her story and asked the crow if he had seen Kay.

'Possibly,' replied the crow, 'possibly.'

'What do you mean?' cried Gerda, and she seized the crow and almost squeezed him to death in her excitement. 'Have you really seen him?'

'Gently, gently!' protested the crow. 'I am not sure if it is Kay or not, but if it is he has certainly forsaken you for his princess.'

'Oh! Is he living with a princess?'

'Wait a bit, wait a bit!' said the crow. 'I find your language so intolerably difficult! Do you not understand crows' language?'

'I'm afraid I have never learnt it,' replied Gerda.

'Never mind,' said the crow. 'I shall have to explain to

you as best I can.' And this is what he had to tell.

'In this kingdom there lives a princess who is extremely intelligent. It is said that she reads all the newspapers in the whole world. Shortly after she ascended the throne she began to wish she had someone to share her responsibilities, so she thought she would like to get married. This was a good idea, but she was determined to marry a man who could take part in good, intelligent conversation – a man who was interesting to talk to, rather than handsome and distinguished. So she called all her ladies-in-waiting together and announced her decision. "What a wonderful idea!" they exclaimed. "We should like to get married too." I assure you I am telling the truth,' said the crow. 'I have a lady-friend who is a tame crow in the palace and she tells me everything that goes on there.

'Advertisements began to appear in all the newspapers, to the effect that every good-looking young man would be welcome at the palace, and that the princess proposed to select as her husband the young man whose conversation she found most entertaining. Well,' said the crow, 'I can assure you that young men hastened to the palace from all over the place – hundreds of them – but they all seemed to be struck dumb before the princess. No matter how brightly they chattered away in the streets, they seemed to lose the power of speech as soon as they came through the palace gates, past the sentries in their silver uniforms and past the gold-clad footmen on the great staircase. There they would stand, gaping stupidly up at the princess, with not a word to say for themselves. The odd thing was that they could talk well enough as soon as they came out of the palace again!

'What an extraordinary spectacle it was to see the hundreds of suitors queuing up along the royal avenue which led from the city gates to the palace! I went along to have a look at them, and a comical sight it was! Hundreds of them there were, all hungry and thirsty, for few of them had brought any food with them. Indeed, they had not expected such a long wait.'

'But what about Kay?' asked Gerda impatiently. 'Was he amongst them?'

'Patience, my dear, patience!' replied the crow. 'I am just coming to him. On the third day, when the crowd of suitors had faded away, a little fellow marched boldly up to the palace, with neither horse nor carriage. His eyes sparkled like yours and he had beautiful long hair, but he was poorly dressed.'

'That was Kay,' sighed Gerda. 'Oh, I have found him after all!' And she clapped her hands for joy.

'He carried a rucksack on his back,' said the crow.

'I think it must have been his sledge,' cried Gerda. 'He went away with his sledge.'

'Possibly,' replied the crow. 'I did not examine it very closely. But my lady-friend tells me that he showed no sign of embarrassment as he strode past the silver-clad sentries and the golden-uniformed footmen. On the contrary, he nodded, he nodded gaily to them and poked them in the ribs, saying, "How boring it must be to stand here all day long. I think I'll go in".'

'The great halls were brilliantly lit. Ministers and servants went to and fro, bare-foot, carrying golden dishes, and the magnificence of the scene was enough to take your breath away. To crown all, the little fellow's shoes squeaked most dreadfully, but oddly enough he showed not the slightest trace of embarrassment.'

'It must have been Kay,' said Gerda. 'I know he had new shoes, for I heard them squeaking in Grandmother's room.'

'Oh yes, they squeaked,' said the crow. 'But he went straight up to the princess, who was sitting on a pearl as big as a spinning-wheel, surrounded by her ladies-in-waiting and their maids and the maids' maids, and all her courtiers and their servants and the servants' servants, who in their turn had servants – and the nearer the door they stood, the more toffee-nosed they were. You would hardly dare to look at the servant's servant standing at the door in his long white stockings!'

'It must have been frightful,' said little Gerda. 'And did Kay win the princess?'

'Aha! My lady-friend told me all about it. He told the princess that he had not come to woo her, but to find out if she was really as clever as she thought! As it happened, they both liked each other immensely, and the princess was most impressed by his intelligence and ready wit.'

'Yes, Kay is clever,' said Gerda. 'He can even work out complicated sums in his head. Please,' she added, 'can you not smuggle me into the palace somehow?'

'That is more easily said than done,' said the crow. 'I must have a word with my lady-friend about it, but, as far as I know, the regulations are strict, and you will never be able to enter the palace openly.'

'Surely it won't be as difficult as all that?' said Gerda. 'When Kay knows I am here he will come out and fetch me in himself.'

'Wait for me by the railing,' said the crow, as he ruffled his wing feathers and flew away.

He did not return till it was growing dark. 'Caw! Caw!' he said. 'My lady-friend sends you greetings, as well as this piece of bread which she filched from the kitchen for you. You must surely be hungry! It is no use, you cannot enter the castle. You don't even have shoes on, and neither the silver sentries nor the golden footmen would ever let you pass. But do not give up hope! My lady-friend knows of a little back staircase which leads directly to the royal chamber, and she thinks she can find the key.'

Gerda and the crow crossed the garden to the great avenue where the leaves were falling. When the lights in the palace had gone out, the crow led Gerda to the little back door, which they found ajar. How Gerda's heart beat with fear and joy! She felt very guilty, although all she wanted was to know whether Kay was alive and well. Surely he must be there! Already she could see his bright eyes and his long hair in her imagination, and saw him smile at her as he had done so long ago under the roses. Surely he would be glad to see her again and to have news of his home? How she trembled with fear and joy!

They had now reached the staircase. It was dimly lit by a lantern on top of a cupboard, and there stood the tame crow, glancing about her and looking Gerda up and down. Gerda curtsied, just as her grandmother had taught her.

'My dear,' said the tame crow, 'I have heard so much about you. I am only too delighted to be able to help you. Take the lamp and follow me – we are unlikely to meet anyone this way.'

'I am sure we are being followed,' said Gerda a moment later. And, indeed, shadows swept past her on the wall – thin-legged horses with flowing manes, huntsmen, lords and ladies on horseback.

'Do not worry,' said the crow. 'They are only dreams. They always haunt the palace at night. They will not harm you.'

They entered the first room. The walls were covered with rose-pink satin embroidered all over with flowers.

They went from room to room, each more magnificent than the last, until they came to the royal bed-chamber, which was so beautiful that it almost took Gerda's breath away. The central pillar was like a golden palm-tree with graceful glass leaves that covered the ceiling. A pair of beautiful beds hung on either side, suspended from golden branches and shaped like lilies. One bed was white and in it lay the princess. The other was crimson, and Gerda supposed she would find Kay sleeping in it.

She stepped softly forward and pushed aside one of the red lily petals. She saw a sun-tanned neck. It must be Kay! She called his name aloud and held up the lamp – a cavalcade of dreams came galloping into the room. The young prince blinked his eyes and sat up – but it was not Kay! He looked like Kay only from behind, but he was still very handsome.

The princess now peeped out from her bed of lily petals and asked what was the matter. Little Gerda burst into tears and told the whole sad story between sobs, not omitting to tell how the crows had tried to help her.

'Poor child!' said the prince and princess, and they praised the crows for being so helpful and promised them a reward. 'Would you like to fly away free to the woods,' asked the princess, 'or would you rather stay here as royal crows, with full rights to everything that falls to the kitchen floor?'

Both crows bowed low and said they would like to stay on at court, for they were thinking of their old age and how pleasant it would be to have all their food provided without having to go and hunt for it.

The prince offered Gerda his crimson lily bed for the night. He could have thought of nothing more fitting for her. 'How kind people are!' thought Gerda. 'How unselfish!' With this pleasant thought she closed her eyes and slept. The dreams all returned with a mighty rush, and appeared to Gerda in the form of angels pulling a little sledge on which Kay sat and nodded to her, but when she awoke they had all disappeared.

Next morning Gerda was dressed from head to foot in

silk and velvet. She was invited to stay at the palace for as long as she wished, but she asked her kind hosts for a little pony-trap with a pony to pull it, and a pair of boots so that she could continue on her way in search of Kay. She was given the boots and a muff, and as soon as she was ready, a golden coach came rolling up to the door, bearing the royal coat-of-arms. The coachman, the footman and the outriders – for there were even outriders – all wore golden crowns. The prince and princess themselves helped her into the coach, and wished her a successful journey.

The crow from the woods, who had married his lady-friend in the meantime, accompanied Gerda for the first few miles. The other crow stood at the door and flapped her wings; she preferred to stay at the palace, for she had a headache as a result of over-eating since her appointment as royal crow.

'Farewell!' cried the prince and princess, and Gerda wept and the crow with her. They travelled the first few miles and then the crow too, bade her farewell. And this was the most painful leave-taking. The crow hopped on to a high branch and flapped his wings at her for as long as he could see the coach glinting in the bright sunshine.

Fifth Story

THE LITTLE ROBBER–GIRL

They drove on through the gloomy forest and the coach shone like a torch. This caught the eye of the robbers and drove them wild with greed.

'It is gold, pure gold!' they cried, and they fell on the coach, seized the horses by the bridles, killed the coachman, the footman and the outriders, and dragged little Gerda from the coach.

'Oh, she is plump and pretty!' exclaimed the horrid old robber-woman, who had a long shaggy beard, and eyebrows which hung down over her eyes. 'She has been well fed on nuts and other good food! She is just like a fat little lamb, ready for slaughter! What a tasty morsel she will be!' And the old woman drew from her belt a bright, shiny knife which flashed horribly in the sunlight.

'Ow,' shrieked the woman, at the very same moment. Her own little daughter, whom she was carrying on her back, had bitten her ear. 'You naughty child!' cried the mother. And so she had no time to kill Gerda.

'I want to play with her!' said the little robber-girl. 'I want her muff and her fine clothes, and she is to share my bed with me.' And she bit her mother again, this time in the other ear, so that the robber-woman leapt in the air and danced about in circles. All the other robbers laughed and called out, 'Just look at her dancing with her little girl!'

'I want to ride in the coach!' cried the robber-girl, and she was so vicious and self-willed that no one dared gainsay her.

She climbed in and made Gerda sit beside her. Off they clattered over roots and boulders, deeper and deeper into the wood. The robber-girl was the same age as Gerda, but stronger and broader in the shoulders, and her skin was much darker. Her eyes were deep black and had an almost melancholy expression. 'They shall not kill you as long as I am with you.' She put her arms round Gerda's neck. 'Are you a real princess?'

'No,' replied Gerda, and she told her story and explained how she loved little Kay.

The robber-girl peered earnestly into Gerda's eyes,

193

nodded, dried Gerda's tears and tucked both hands into her muff, which was beautifully warm.

Suddenly the coach came to a halt in the courtyard of the robbers' castle. The walls of the castle were crumbling, and ravens and crows flew in and out of the gaping holes. Enormous dogs, which looked big enough to swallow a man at one gulp, leapt up at the coach, baring their teeth, but not a sound came from their throats, for they had been trained not to bark.

A huge fire was burning on the stone flags of the old hall, whose walls and ceiling were blackened with smoke. There was no chimney and the smoke drifted round the hall till it found a crack through which it could escape. A great pot of soup was suspended over the flames, and hares and rabbits were roasting on spits.

'This evening you are to sleep with me and my animals,' announced the robber-girl.

They ate and drank together and then retired to a corner, where a pile of straw and rough blankets lay. On the rafters above them perched well over a hundred doves, which seemed to be asleep, though many of them stirred as the girls approached.

'They are all mine,' declared the robber-girl. She seized the nearest dove and held it upside down by the legs, letting it flap and struggle. 'Kiss it!' And she held it up to Gerda's face. 'The wood pigeons stay up there,' she added, pointing to a barred hole in the wall. 'They would fly away if I did not keep them well shut up. And here is Bo, my special pet.' She dragged forward a reindeer by its antlers, and Gerda saw that the poor beast was fettered and had a heavy copper ring round its neck. 'I tickle his throat with my sharp hunting-knife every evening, just to make sure he is afraid of me.'

With these words the girl drew a long knife from a

crack in the wall and ran its point across the reindeer's throat. The poor beast kicked and bucked, and the robber-girl laughed and pulled Gerda over to her bed.

'Do you take your knife to bed with you?' asked Gerda, looking at the girl fearfully.

'Oh yes. You never know what might happen. But tell me all about Kay, and about your adventures.'

So Gerda told her story. From the hole in the wall high above them came the incessant cooing of pigeons, which soon lulled the little robber-girl to sleep, with one arm round Gerda's neck and the other tightly clasping her knife.

Not a wink of sleep came to Gerda, for she was much too frightened. The robbers squatted round the great fire, eating and drinking, while the old robber-woman turned somersaults on the floor. It was dreadful!

'Coo, coo,' said the wood pigeons. 'We have seen little Kay. A white hen was drawing his sledge, but he was sitting with the Snow Queen in her sleigh. She drove through our wood when we were tiny chicks in the nest. Her breath was so cold that all the young pigeons froze to death – we two were the only survivors. Coo, coo!'

'Where was the Snow Queen going?' cried Gerda. 'Can't you tell me any more?'

'She must have been going to Lapland, where there's nothing but snow and ice. Ask the reindeer – he is sure to know.'

'Oh yes,' said the reindeer, 'Lapland is a fine country, plenty of beautiful snow and ice. There you can roam about through the broad, gleaming valleys! That is where the Snow Queen has her summer tent. Her castle is much further on towards the North Pole.'

'Oh, Kay, dear Kay!' sobbed Gerda.

'Lie still,' said the robber-girl, 'or you'll get my knife in your belly!'

Next morning Gerda repeated what the wood pigeons had said, and the robber-girl looked serious for a moment. Then, turning to the reindeer, she asked, 'Do you know where Lapland is?'

'I ought to know Lapland,' he replied, with an eager gleam in his eyes. 'I was born and bred there, and all my childhood days were spent romping about on the snowfields.'

'All right,' said the robber-girl. 'As you see, most of our men are away at present. Only Mother is there, and she has been drinking from the big flask and she is sure to doze off soon. The moment she is asleep I will do something to help you.'

She leapt out of bed and flung her arms round her mother's neck, tweaked her beard, and said, 'Good morning, my dear, sweet old goat!' And her mother gave her a cuff that made her nose black and blue. But it was all in play.

As soon as her mother had taken another drink from the bottle and drowsed off to sleep, the robber-girl took her sharp knife and went up to the reindeer. 'I should dearly like to keep you here, so that I could amuse myself by tickling your throat with this big knife. But instead, I am going to cut your rope and send you off to Lapland. How does that suit you? But you must work for your freedom. I want you to take this little girl to the Snow Queen's castle and help her to find her friend. I know you were listening when she told her story, so you know what to do.'

The reindeer leapt for joy and would hardly stand still for long enough to allow Gerda to climb on to his back. The robber-girl tied her on to make her more secure and even gave her a cushion to sit on.

'Here are your fur boots,' she said. 'You will need them in all that cold. But I will keep your muff – it is so soft. But, never mind, you won't freeze! Here are Mother's long gloves.'

Gerda wept for joy.

'What's the matter?' asked the robber-girl. 'Aren't you pleased? Here are two loaves and a piece of ham so that you don't starve.' And she tied them all to the reindeer's back. When she was sure that everything was safe, she opened the door and called away the great dogs which were crouching outside. Then she cut through the rope with her knife and said to the reindeer, 'Off you go now, but mind you look after the little girl!'

Gerda stretched out her hands in the huge gloves to the robber-girl and said goodbye.

Away they flew over mountain and valley, through great forests, across marshes and plains, but the reindeer hardly stopped to recover his breath. Around them wolves howled and ravens croaked, and fiery lights appeared in the sky.

'Those are my beloved old Northern Lights!' said the reindeer. 'See how the whole sky is aglow!'

On and on they ran, day and night. When the bread and ham were finished they reached Lapland.

Sixth Story

THE LAPP WOMAN AND THE FINNISH WOMAN

They came to a halt outside a wretched little hut. Its roof very nearly touched the ground, and the door was so low that Gerda had to crawl in on her hands and knees. There was no one in the hut except an old Lapp woman, who was busy cooking fish over an oil lamp. The reindeer told her Gerda's story, but not before he had told his own, which he considered of much greater importance. Poor Gerda was so numbed with the cold that she could not speak.

'You poor things!' exclaimed the woman. 'You have many miles yet to go before you reach Finland. That is where the Snow Queen lives and spends the long dark nights burning strange fireworks. I will write a few lines on a dried cod – for I have no paper – for you to give to an old Finnish woman. She will be much better able to help you than I am.'

When Gerda had warmed herself and had eaten and drunk, and the woman had written her note on a dried cod, she set off again with the reindeer. All night long the sky glowed with the beautiful blue Northern Lights. At last they came to Finland and knocked on the chimney of the Finnish woman's house, for there was no door.

Inside the house it was so warm that the old woman wore almost no clothes. She was wizened and ugly, but hospitable. She helped Gerda off with all her warm clothes and her long gloves and boots, for otherwise she would have been far too hot, and laid a block of ice on the reindeer's head. Then she read the message that was written on the dried cod. Three times she read it, till she knew it off by heart; then she threw the cod into the pot to cook. There was little food to be had in this far northern land, so nothing must be wasted!

Once again the reindeer told his own story to begin with, then Gerda's, and the woman blinked her wise old eyes slowly, but said not a word.

'I know how clever you are,' said the reindeer. 'I know that you bind all the winds of the world with a single thread. If the sailor loosens the first knot, he gets a fair wind; if he unties the second, a strong wind; if he unties the third and fourth knots, there is such a gale that whole forests are uprooted. Can you give this little girl a potion that will give her the strength of twelve men, and enable her to overcome the Snow Queen?'

'The strength of twelve men ...' mused the old woman. 'I wonder if that would help.' She went to a shelf and took down a large roll of dried animal skins.

She unwrapped them and began to study, for they were covered with strange writing. So intent was her concentration that sweat began to pour from her brow.

Meantime Gerda sat in her corner with tears in her eyes, not knowing what she should do. Suddenly the old woman's eyes began to twinkle, and she drew the reindeer aside into the opposite corner. She laid a fresh block of ice on his head and whispered softly, 'Little Kay is in the Snow Queen's palace. He has everything he can possibly want and thinks it is the most wonderful place in the whole world. But that is due to the glass splinters in his eye and his heart. Until they are removed it is hard to see how he can remember his family and friends or, indeed, how he can think of anything but the Snow Queen and her palace. He is well and truly in her power.'

'But can you not give little Gerda something that will enable her to win Kay back from the Snow Queen?'

'I can give her no greater power than she already possesses. Can you not see how all creatures seem to serve her, and how she has come unharmed over such vast distances? Her power is greater than ours, for it lies in her generous and unselfish heart – the heart of a loving and innocent child. If she is unable to penetrate the Snow Queen's palace and free Kay from the glass splinters on her own, I am quite certain we cannot do it for her. The Snow Queen's estate begins two miles from here. Take her there and set her down beside the great bush with the red berries that is growing in the snow. Say not a word, but hasten back here without wasting a moment.'

And the Finnish woman lifted Gerda on to the reindeer's back, and off they went at a gallop.

'Oh, I have left my gloves and boots behind!' cried

Gerda, as soon as she felt the biting cold. But the reindeer would not stop and sped on and on over snow and
ice until they reached the bush with the red berries.
There he set her down and kissed her on the mouth, and
big tears trickled down his cheeks. Then he galloped
away at great speed, soon vanishing into the white world.

There stood poor Gerda in the middle of icy-cold Finland without gloves and without boots. She began to run
on as fast as she could. Suddenly a whole regiment of
snowflakes advanced upon her, but these had not fallen
from the sky, for it was clear and shone in the gleam of
the Northern Lights. No, these snowflakes came straight
towards her on the ground, and as they came they
seemed to fuse and take on strange and terrible forms.
Gerda remembered how beautiful the snowflakes at
home had looked under the magnifying glass, but
these were quite different – much bigger, and ugly and
terrifying to look at. They were the Snow Queen's
guards, and the shapes they took on as they formed and
reformed were many and varied. There were some like
hideous great hedgehogs, some like clusters of snakes
with heads waving in all directions, and others like small
fat bears with bristling fur. And they were all dazzling
white – living snowflakes.

Little Gerda began to pray, and asked God for
strength and courage. The cold was so intense that the
breath came from her mouth like a column of smoke.
And her breath became thicker and thicker and finally
formed into little transparent angels, which grew bigger
and bigger as they neared the ground. All had helmets
on their heads and shields and spears ready in their
hands. The bodyguard became more and more numerous until Gerda found herself surrounded by a whole
army of angels. They advanced against the gigantic

snowflakes of the Snow Queen, and shattered them into a thousand pieces with their spears. So Gerda walked on towards the Snow Queen's palace, and as she walked the angels stroked her bare hands and feet with their wings, sending warm blood pulsing through her veins once more.

But now we must see what Kay is doing. Is he thinking of Gerda? Has he the faintest suspicion that she is standing outside at the castle gates?

Seventh Story

THE SNOW QUEEN'S PALACE

The palace walls were of driving snow, the doors and windows of biting winds. There were more than a hundred great halls, of which the biggest was many miles from side to side. All were brilliantly lit by strong Northern Lights. How vast, how empty, how icy and how glittering they were! No happy parties were ever seen within these walls, not even a ball for the polar bears so that they could dance to the music of the four winds; there was no one to play the fool there, not even a little coffee party for the white foxes as an excuse to gossip. And over it all shone the Northern Lights – beautiful and clear, but cold and hard, without a ray of life-giving warmth.

In the middle of the vast snow hall was a frozen lake. The ice was broken into thousands of pieces, but each piece was so like the others that they might all have been made from a pattern. And in the middle of this lake was the Snow Queen's throne where she sat when she was at home, secure in the knowledge of her own grandeur and magnificence.

Little Kay was blue with cold, but he felt nothing, for the Snow Queen had kissed away all his sense of cold and his heart was a lump of ice. To and fro he ran with the triangular fragments of ice, trying desperately to make something, as with a jigsaw puzzle. He had made a great many curious shapes which demanded considerable skill; for Kay was clever, and the glass fragment in his eye had, if anything, increased his intelligence. He even formed whole words, but one word he could never form, and that was 'Eternity'. The Snow Queen had said to him, 'If you can make this word, I will make you master of the whole world, and give you a new pair of skates as well.' But she knew he could not do it.

'Now I will fly to the warm south,' said the Snow Queen. 'I must have a look at the black craters of Mount Etna and Vesuvius and sprinkle a little snow round the edges. It is good for the vineyards and orange groves below.'

And away she flew, leaving Kay alone in the vast hall of ice.

He gazed at the ice fragments and thought and thought, concentrating so hard that his frozen heart cracked. Stiff and motionless he sat, looking as ice-bound as the great white hall around him.

At this moment Gerda came in through the palace gates. A bitter gust of wind almost blew her back again, but she prayed and the wind died down as if by magic. She advanced through room after room, till she came to the great hall with the frozen lake.

As soon as she saw Kay she flew to him and flung her arms about his neck, crying, 'My dearest Kay, I have found you at last!'

But not a sound came from his lips. He sat motionless,

cold and stiff. Gerda began to sob, and her warm tears fell on Kay's chest, penetrated right into his heart, and the lump of ice began to melt. Kay looked at her with a puzzled expression in his eyes, and Gerda felt hope stir within her. A sad, sweet smile filled her tearful eyes as she sang him the song which they used to sing so long ago as they sat together under the roses in the window garden.

The result was unexpected, for it was now Kay's turn to burst into tears, and they flowed so freely that they washed the glass splinter from his eye. He recognized Gerda immediately and exclaimed with joy, 'My dear little Gerda, what has been wrong with me all this time? Have I been ill? How cold it is here!' And he looked about him. 'How lonely and empty!'

He flung his arms round Gerda's neck, and she hardly knew whether to laugh or cry. They were both so perfectly happy that even the ice fragments danced for joy, and when they were tired of dancing they sank down of their own accord to form the word 'Eternity', which the Snow Queen had required of Kay before he could regain his liberty and become his own lord and master.

Gerda kissed Kay's cheeks and they began to glow with rosy health; she kissed his eyes and they began to sparkle like her own; she kissed his hands and feet, and the life returned to them. No matter now when the Snow Queen chose to return – the magic word lay there at his feet in glinting icy letters.

They held hands and walked out through the palace door, and wherever they went the wind died down and the sun came out. When they reached the bush with the red berries they found the reindeer waiting for them with a young female reindeer, whose udders were full of fresh warm milk, which she gladly gave to refresh the children. Then they rode without delay to the old Finnish woman's hut, where they warmed themselves beside the stove before setting out for the Lapp woman's hut. They found that she had been busy sewing warm clothes for them, and had even made ready a sledge.

Kay and Gerda now said goodbye sadly to their reindeer friend and to the Lapp woman. The first young birds began to twitter and the forest was full of green buds.

Suddenly they heard the pounding of hooves, and a superb horse appeared. Gerda knew it at once – it was one of the horses which had been harnessed to her golden coach. On its back rode the little robber-girl, with a red cap on her head and a pair of pistols tucked into her belt. She had grown tired of life with the robbers and was going into the wide world to see what was to be seen and what adventures were to be found. How glad they were to see each other again!

'A fine young fellow you are!' said the robber-girl to Kay. 'I cannot think why Gerda bothered to scour the world for you.'

But Gerda stroked Kay's cheek and asked for news of the prince and princess.

'They have gone to foreign lands,' replied the girl.

'And the crow?' asked Gerda.

'Dead,' was the reply. 'I'm afraid the tame crow is a widow now and hops about with a black ribbon round her leg. She makes a great show of mourning, but she is not really unhappy. But tell me about yourself. I want to know all that happened to you and how you found your friend.'

So Gerda and Kay told the whole story, and when it

was time to part the robber-girl promised to visit them in town some day. For the present, however, she was determined to seek more exciting adventures, so off she rode while Kay and Gerda continued on their way, hand in hand.

Wherever they went they found spring flowers peeping through the grass and the buds on the trees bursting into leaf. They heard church bells ringing, and recognized the houses and tall spires of their own city. They ran through the city gates to Grandmother's house and hurried up the stairs and into the attic room, where they found everything exactly as they had left it. Not a thing had changed. The clock ticked softly and the hands turned. But as they stood in the doorway it suddenly dawned on them that they had grown up.

The roses in the roof garden nodded in at the window and, outside, the little chairs still stood in their shade. Hand in hand Kay and Gerda sat down in the sunshine. The cold, empty magnificence of the Snow Queen lay safely behind them like a bad dream. Grandmother sat in the sun by the window and read aloud from the Bible. 'Unless you become as little children, you cannot enter the Kingdom of God.'

Kay and Gerda gazed into each other's eyes, squeezed each other's hands and smiled. There they sat, grown-up, yet children, children at heart, and it was summer, warm, glorious, blessed summer.

The Cold Heart

No one travelling through Swabia should forget to have a look at the Black Forest, not only because of the trees – although you will find any number of magnificent, tall pine trees there – but also because of the people, who are entirely different from those of the valleys round about. They are abnormally tall, broad-shouldered and of powerful build, almost as if the invigorating scent of the pine needles had endowed them with a certain rude courage, a stronger pair of lungs and a clearer pair of eyes than are enjoyed by the inhabitants of the surrounding plains and valleys. Those who live in the Baden side of the Black Forest wear particularly colourful clothes; the men never shave, but allow their beards to grow as nature intended they should. Their thick, black, close-fitting jackets, their wide, pleated breeches, their red stockings and their wide-brimmed, high-crowned hats render their appearance a little unusual, yet serious and distinguished. The main occupation in this part of the forest is glass-making, but the people are also renowned for their clocks, which they sell over half the world.

The people who live on the other side of the forest are related to the glass-makers, but their occupation has given them quite different customs and traditions. They make their living from the forest itself, for they fell and hew the great pines and float them down the River Nagold to the Neckar, and thence into the Rhine, which takes them right down to Holland; even at the coast the people of the Black Forest are well known for their long rafts of logs. In every city through which the river passes they stop and wait proudly for customers to come and buy their timber; their best customers, however, are the Dutch mynheers, who buy their longest and strongest trees for building ships.

These folk are accustomed to a rough open-air life, and their Sunday dress is quite different from that of the glass-makers on the other side of the forest. They wear dark linen jackets, open down the front, green braces fastened across their broad chests, and black leather trousers, with a rule of brass protruding from the pocket like a badge of honour. Their boots are their pride and joy, for they are probably the biggest to be found anywhere in the world. They can be pulled right up above the knees to the top of the thighs, and the raftsmen can wade about in three feet of water with the greatest of ease without wetting their feet.

Not so very long ago the inhabitants of this forest believed in woodland spirits, and it is only in recent years that the superstition has shown signs of dying out. The odd thing is that even the woodland spirits seemed to dress in the correct costume for the part of the Black Forest they haunted. There was evidence that the Glass Manikin – a little fellow barely four feet high – always appeared in a wide-brimmed, high-crowned hat, wearing a close-fitting jacket, wide breeches and red stockings. But Dutch Michael, who was to be seen on the other side of the forest, was said to be a gigantic, broad-shouldered fellow, dressed in the garb of a raftsman.

A certain young man once had a strange adventure with both of these woodland spirits. Let me tell you about it.

There lived in the Black Forest a widow, Frau Barbara Munk, whose husband had been a charcoal burner.

After his death she was left to bring up her ten-year-old son in the same trade. Young Peter Munk was a slim fellow, who at first was quite content to sit and tend his charcoal-kiln day after day, week after week, month after month, for after all he had never seen anything else of life when his father had been alive. When he was not watching the smoke seep lazily from the kiln, he was down in the villages and towns of the valley selling his charcoal. But a charcoal-burner has plenty of time to think about himself and others, and when Peter Munk sat by his kiln the shadowy trees and the unbroken silence of the forest moved his heart to tears and filled him with a strange longing. At first he had no idea what was the matter, but gradually he began to realize what it was that troubled him – his way of life. 'A black, lonely charcoal-burner!' he mused. 'What a wretched life this is! How much more respected are the glass-makers, the clock-makers, even Sunday-night musicians! Even when I scrub myself and comb my hair and wear father's dress jacket with silver buttons down the front and my brand new red stockings, what good is it? "I wonder who this slim young fellow can be?" people say when they come up behind me, and they admire my stockings and my fine bearing. But as soon as they see my face, they always add, "Oh, it's only Peter Munk the charcoal-burner!"'

Even the raftsmen on the other side of the forest made him envious. From time to time these enormous fellows would come across the forest for a dance or a party, and a fine-looking crowd they were, swearing away in Dutch and smoking clay pipes a yard long, just like the myn-heers of Holland. Then Peter used to think that to be a raftsman must be the most wonderful life in the world! After all, these fellows had only to dig their hands into their pockets to pull out a whole handful of golden dollars, and it was unbelievable to see how much money changed hands when they played dice! Then he would finger the few pence in his own pocket and slink miserably home to his hut.

There were three raftsmen he particularly admired. One of them was a powerful, heavily built man with a red face, who was said to be the richest man in the forest. He was called Big Ezekiel. Twice a year he took a raft of logs down the river to Amsterdam, and somehow his timber always managed to fetch higher prices than anyone else's, with the result that, while all the others walked home, he would ride. The second man was very tall and thin as a rake, and was known throughout the forest as Skinny Willy. Peter envied him his extraordinary audacity; he was outspoken with even the most eminent people, no matter whom he was addressing. At the inn he took up more room than four normal people, for he would sprawl over the table on his elbows, or put one of his long legs up on the bench so that no one could sit beside him – and no one dared to argue with him, for he was extremely rich and powerful. The third was a good-looking young man, who was the best dancer for miles around and was called King of the Dance-floor. He had once been poor, serving his apprenticeship to a woodman, but quite suddenly he had become enormously rich, and it was said that he had unearthed a pot of gold while felling a tree; but others claimed that he had fished up a sack of gold coins from the Rhine with one of the long spiked poles the raftsmen used for fishing. Undoubtedly the gold must have been part of the treasure of the Nibelungs, who were known to have hidden it in the Rhine.

As he sat all alone in the pine forests Peter would often

think of these three men. Admittedly they were all disliked because of their greed and their harsh treatment of their debtors, but the world is a strange place, for while they were despised for their greed they were at the same time respected for their wealth.

'It's no use!' Peter sighed in despair one day, as he sat with his chin cupped in his hands. The previous day had been a holiday and everyone from miles around had been at the inn. 'If I don't make a lucky strike soon I shall do something desperate!' He racked his brains to think of some means of making money quickly, but no ideas came to him.

At last he remembered the forest legend about people who had suddenly become rich with the help of Dutch Michael and the Glass Manikin. He could almost remember the verse which was supposed to summon the Glass Manikin to appear on the pine-tree hill in the middle of the forest. It began:

> Guardian of the forest treasure,
> Watchman here for many a year,
> Do your utmost for my pleasure . . .

But there he stuck. He thought and thought, but the last line completely escaped him. He often thought of asking some of the oldest inhabitants for the last line, but somehow he always held back at the last minute.

Eventually he spoke to his mother about the Glass Manikin, but she could tell him only what he knew already, and she could remember no more than the first line of the verse. What she did say, however, was that only those who had been born on a Sunday between eleven and two o'clock could ever see the little man, and that Peter would be well qualified if only he knew the verse, for he had been born at midday on a Sunday.

This news made Peter jump for joy, and he determined to see what could be done, even without the last line of the verse. So one day when he had finished selling his charcoal he allowed his kiln to go out, put on his father's jacket with the silver buttons, a brand new pair of red stockings and his Sunday hat, took his five-foot black-thorn staff and set out for the pine-tree hill.

This hill was the highest in the whole forest, miles from anywhere – there was no human habitation for miles in any direction. Seldom did anyone try to fell timber in that area, for those who had made the attempt had almost always done themselves harm. Many were the stories of axe-blows glancing off tree-trunks and chopping off the woodman's toes or, worse still, of trees crashing down too quickly and in the wrong direction, crushing the woodman as they fell. And so it came about that the trees on this hill were thicker and taller than anywhere else in the forest, with the result that even in broad daylight the forest was almost as dark as night, and Peter trembled as he groped and stumbled his way slowly and cautiously uphill. There was no voice to be heard, no footstep other than his own, and no sound of axe on wood. Even the birds seemed to avoid this part of the forest.

Suddenly he was confronted by the most enormous pine he had ever seen, and realized that he had reached the top of the hill. Surely this is where the guardian of the treasure will live? he thought. He swept off his hat and bowed deeply before the tree, cleared his throat and said without a quiver in his voice, 'Good evening, Mr Glassman.' There was no answer, and the forest was as silent as ever. Perhaps he should repeat the verse, he thought, so he murmured:

'Guardian of the forest treasure,
Watchman here for many a year,
Do your utmost for my pleasure . . .'

As he spoke these words he was thrilled and at the same time terrified to see a strange little fellow peep out from behind the giant pine tree, looking exactly as he had always heard the Glass Manikin described. The black jacket, the little red stockings and the pointed hat, even the pale but smiling and clear-cut features seemed exactly right. But, alas, as suddenly as he had appeared the Glass Manikin vanished again!

'Please, Mr Glassman,' called Peter, after a moment's hesitation, 'please do not tease me! Mr Glassman! Don't think I did not see you – I saw you quite plainly, peeping round the tree!' There was no reply, but he was sure that he heard a faint chuckling behind the tree. Peter shook his head. He knew that he had not completed the verse and that this must be why the manikin had disappeared, but no matter how hard he thought he could not remember the last line.

He walked round and round the tree, but not a trace of the little man could he find. Suddenly he grew frightened and he began to run, and as he ran the trees seemed to close in, thicker and darker than ever, almost as if they were trying to catch him. This terrified him and he took to his heels and fled. He went on running until he heard dogs barking in the distance and saw smoke winding up through the trees. It came from a woodman's hut, for in his haste Peter had come down the wrong side of the hill into the territory of the woodmen and raftsmen.

In the hut dwelt an old man, his son and his son's wife, and a number of grandchildren. They were only too

pleased to offer Peter a bed for the night, for life was lonely in the forest and visitors were few. They gave him a mug of cider to drink, and for supper they had a roast capercailzie – a dish for which the Black Forest is famous.

After supper the wife and girls sat with their sewing and weaving under the great oil-lamp in the middle of the room, which the youngest girls fed from time to time with fine pine resin. The men sat and smoked their long clay pipes, while the boys carved forks and spoons out of hardwood.

A storm was building up outside, for the wind howled and the pines creaked and groaned, and sometimes it sounded almost as if whole trees were being snapped off by a giant hand and hurled to the ground. The children wanted to go outside to watch the violent play of the elements, but their grandfather warned them against it. 'It is as much as your life is worth to show your face outside that door tonight,' he said. 'Dutch Michael is busy in the forest, cutting timber for a new raft.'

The boys stared at him. They had heard of Dutch Michael often enough, but they did not really believe in him; however, they asked the old man to tell them all about Michael. Peter was only too eager to hear the story, for though he had heard people talk of Dutch Michael he wanted to know more about him. 'He is the master of this wood,' said the old man. 'I will tell you how the story began. About a hundred years ago, so my grandfather told me, there were no more honourable or warm-hearted folk anywhere in the world than the people of the Black Forest. Nowadays there is far too much money about, and the people have become grasping and unreliable. It was different in those days, and even if he were to look in at the window this very minute, I would say to his face that Dutch Michael is responsible for all the dishonesty and corruption that is rife in the forest.

'Well, a century ago there lived a good, honest wood-merchant who employed many assistants. He traded on both banks of the Rhine for many miles down-river, and his business flourished, for he was a good man. One evening a man came to his door, the like of whom had never been seen before. He was dressed exactly as any other Black Forest woodman, but he was a good foot taller than anyone ever seen in the forest before or since. He was a giant of a man. He asked for work, and the merchant quickly agreed on a wage and engaged him on the spot.

'Never before had there been such a worker! He felled more trees than three ordinary workers and, if six men were carrying the thin end of a tree, he could carry the thick end on his own shoulder with the greatest of ease. After he had worked for six months as a woodman, he went to his master and said, "I have spent long enough chopping wood and I should like to see where my trees are going. Could you not send me down-river with your rafts?"

'So the merchant replied, "I have no wish to stand in your way, Michael, if you want to see a bit of the world. I need strong fellows like you here in the forest, and your great strength may well be wasted on the rafts, but by all means go for at least one journey."

'The raft which he was to accompany consisted of eight parts, with the smallest logs in front and the largest at the rear. What do you think happened on the night before they set off? At the last moment Michael carried another eight enormous logs down to the river, with as much ease as if he had been carrying rafting poles. The strength of the man was terrifying. To this day no one has the least idea where he felled them. The wood-merchant was delighted, for he reckoned they would bring him extra profit, but Michael said, "I need these for steering the raft. Those miserable sticks you use for rafting poles are no use to me."

'They pushed off from the bank, and if Michael had already astounded the woodmen by his prodigious strength, the raftsmen were even more amazed. They naturally expected to make slow progress downstream because of the immense weight of the logs, but as soon as they reached the Neckar they found themselves shooting rapidly downstream, like an arrow from a bow. The bends in the Neckar generally caused a great deal of trouble and many a good raft had been hopelessly stranded for hours on end on a sandbank or stretch of gravel because the raftsmen had been unable to hold it in mid-stream. On this occasion, however, Michael leapt off the raft at each bend or stretch of rapids and pushed or hauled the raft left or right to avoid any danger that threatened. In this way they arrived in record time at Cologne on the Rhine, which is where the timber was normally sold. But up spoke Michael. "What a fine lot of merchants you are! Do you really believe that the people of Cologne need all this wood for themselves? Not a bit of it! How could they use all the wood that comes from the Black Forest? No, they float it on down the Rhine to Holland, where they sell it at double the price they paid for it. Let's sell the small logs here and take the big ones on to Holland. Whatever they fetch above the usual price will be our own profit."

'So spoke the cunning Michael, and the other raftsmen agreed readily enough – some because the idea of a trip to Holland appealed to them, and some simply because they wanted the money. Only a single raftsman was honest enough to warn them against risking their master's property, or at any rate against concealing the true price from him, but no one listened to him and his advice was soon forgotten – except by Dutch Michael, as you will hear! So they carried on down the Rhine until they came at last to Rotterdam, where they sold the timber for four times the price in Cologne, and Michael's heavy logs at the back of the raft fetched a particularly high price. The rafters had never seen so much money before, and were almost speechless when Michael divided it out – three parts for themselves, and one part for their master.

'They soon frittered away their money, for they mingled with sailors and wastrels at the inns and spent vast sums on drink, gambling and other vices. The poor fellow who had so honestly tried to protect his master's interests was sold by Michael to the press-gang and was never heard of again. And from that day on, Holland became a sort of paradise to the raftsmen of the Black Forest, and Dutch Michael a sort of king. For many a long year the honest wood-merchant had no suspicion of what was going on, and money, cursing and swearing, vice, gambling and drunkenness gradually pervaded the forest.

'When at last the story came out Dutch Michael was nowhere to be found, but you may be sure he is not dead. For over a hundred years his spirit has haunted the forest and, if the truth be known, he has helped many people to make their fortunes – but only at the price of their souls. There is no need to say more, but the fact remains that on stormy nights like this he is busy felling the finest and tallest trees on the pine-tree hill, where no one else dares to fell. He gives these to the poor, misguided folk in order to persuade them to turn aside from the straight and narrow path and go to him for help.

'That is the story of Dutch Michael, and there is no doubt that all the evil in the forest can be ascribed to him. True, he can make you rich,' added the old man, lowering his voice almost to a whisper, 'but I would rather accept nothing from him. Not for anything in the world would I be in Big Ezekiel's shoes, or Skinny

Willy's, and I am sure that the Dance-floor King has had dealings with him!'

While the old man had been talking the storm had abated. The women and girls went off to bed, and the men filled a mattress with dried leaves for Peter beside the stove and wished him good night.

Never had Peter dreamt such terrifying dreams as he did that night. At one time he seemed to see Dutch Michael fling open the window and hand him, with his monstrously long arm, a bag of gold coins, which he scattered on the floor like a shower of golden rain. At another time he thought he saw the little Glass Manikin, wreathed in smiles, sailing round and round the room on a big glass bottle; and he seemed to hear the same husky chuckling he had heard on the pine-tree hill; and then it was interrupted by a deep voice booming:

> 'In Holland there's gold
> For those who are bold
> To have and to hold.
> Gold! Gold!'

Then again he would hear the little verse about the guardian in the forest, and a deep, soft voice seemed to whisper in his ear, 'How stupid you are, Peter! Stupid Peter! Stupid! You can't find a rhyme for "year" and yet you were born at midday on a Sunday! Rhyme, Peter, rhyme!'

When he awoke at first flush of dawn he remembered the dream and the soft whisperings in his ear, 'Rhyme, stupid Peter, rhyme!' But no matter how hard he racked his brain, he could think of no suitable rhyme. As he sat, downcast and dejected, trying to find a rhyme for "year", three young men passed through the trees outside the window, singing as they went:

    'To North and South and East and West
     Our forest does appear
    To gather power from the soil
    And grow from year to year.'

Like a flash Peter leapt to his feet. 'That's it!' he almost shouted. 'It must be right! "Appear" rhymes with "year". Well, my little Glass Manikin, perhaps we'll have another word together some time soon.'

He took up his hat and long stick, thanked his hosts for their hospitality and retraced his steps towards the pine-tree hill. Slowly and pensively he strolled along, for he had to think of that last line. What in the world could it be?

Suddenly, just as he was about to ascend the hill where the trees became really thick, he thought of a line that fitted perfectly, and he almost danced for joy. But at that very moment an enormous man, dressed as a raftsman, strode through the trees with a staff as long as a ship's mast in his hand. Peter almost fell to his knees when he saw the giant approaching with measured tread, for he had little doubt that it was Dutch Michael. The man paused and looked down at Peter, but not a word did he speak. The silence became oppressive. He was a good head taller than the tallest man Peter had ever seen. His features were furrowed and wrinkled, although not old; he was wearing a canvas jacket and leather breeches, with huge boots pulled up above his knees. No, there could be no doubt who he was.

'What are you doing here on the pine-tree hill, Peter Munk?' boomed the king of the forest at last, and there was menace in his voice.

'Good morning, kind friend,' replied Peter, doing his utmost to conceal his terror and to put on a bold front, though he could hardly keep a quiver out of his voice. 'I am on the way to my home on the far side of the hill.'

'Do not lie to me, Peter the charcoal burner,' thundered Dutch Michael, 'or I will crush you to pulp with my staff!' Then, in a softer voice, he added, 'Do you think I didn't see you up there, begging from the manikin? That was a silly thing to do, Peter, and it is well for you that you did not know the last line of the verse. He is a mean old skinflint, the little fellow – very niggardly with his gifts and very demanding of those who receive them. Come, Peter, you can surely do better than that! You're a fine young fellow, well able to make a name for yourself in the world, and yet you sit burning charcoal. I am very sorry for you! When other people seem to have money to burn, it is all you can do to produce a few miserable pence at the inn. That's a poor kind of life!'

'That's very true, and you are right. It is a poor kind of life.'

'It all depends what you make of it,' continued Michael. 'I have helped quite a number of men in my time, and you will by no means be the first. It is up to you! Tell me, how much money do you need to begin with?'

With these words he rattled the coins in his enormous money-bag, and it sounded just as it had in the dream. Peter's heart was beating frantically. He grew cold and hot in rapid succession, for Dutch Michael did not look the sort of man to give away something for nothing. Peter remembered what the old woodman had said about the rich men in the forest and, impelled by a sudden inexplicable terror, he cried out, 'Many thanks for the offer, but I know all about you and I want nothing to do with you!'

He took to his heels and ran away as fast as his legs

would carry him, but the huge fellow came pounding along beside him with enormous strides, talking as he ran – and there was a fearful menace in his voice. 'You will regret it, Peter, I can see it written in your face. I can see in your eyes that you cannot escape me. But, listen to reason! Do not run so fast – you'll soon be at my border.'

At that moment Peter spied a narrow green ditch ahead, and he ran faster than ever in an attempt to cross the border before it was too late, with the result that Michael came pounding along even faster behind him, muttering threats and curses as he came. Looking over his shoulder, Peter saw Michael with his staff upraised in order to crush him to pulp, and took a long, desperate leap over the ditch. Just as he landed on the other side the staff shattered into fragments in mid-air as if against an invisible barrier, and a long piece fell at Peter's feet.

Peter bent down and picked it up in order to throw it at Michael, but the moment his hand touched it he felt the wood wriggle in his grasp and saw to his horror that it was an enormous snake with flashing, yellow eyes and flickering tongue, which was already rearing up to strike him. He let go immediately, but by this time it had coiled its body round his arm and the fearsome head was poised for the fatal blow. Peter thought all was lost, when a great capercailzie swooped down through the trees and seized the snake in its beak, just behind the head, and flew off with it. Dutch Michael, who had seen everything from the ditch, screamed with fury and frustration as he saw the snake being carried away by a creature more powerful than himself.

Exhausted and trembling, Peter continued on his way. The track became steeper, the forest wilder, and before long he found himself at the enormous pine tree on the top of the hill. As he had done on the previous day, he bowed towards the invisible Glass Manikin and began:

> 'Guardian of the forest treasure,
> Watchman here for many a year,
> Do your utmost for my pleasure,
> To Sunday's child you must appear.'

'Not quite right, Peter my lad,' said a quiet husky voice near by. 'But we'll let it go as it's you.'

Peter looked round in astonishment and saw a little old man sitting at the foot of a beautiful pine, wearing a black jacket, red stockings and wide-brimmed hat. His features were gentle and kindly, and his beard looked as soft as spun gossamer. Peter was surprised to see him smoking a blue glass pipe, and as he moved closer he could see that his clothes, too, were made of coloured glass, even his shoes and his hat. But the glass was flexible, as if it were still molten, and it bent and wrinkled whenever the little old man moved.

'I see you met that great lout, Dutch Michael!' said the little man in his strange husky voice. 'He must have given you rather a fright, but I spoilt his staff for him, didn't I?'

'Indeed, sir, I was terrified,' admitted Peter. 'You must have been the capercailzie that killed the snake. Many thanks indeed for saving my life. But I came here to ask your advice. I am most unhappy, and I shall never go far in the world as a mere charcoal-burner. I thought that, as I am still young, I might do something better with my life. I see plenty of folk around me who do well for themselves in a remarkably short time – for example, Big Ezekiel and the Dance-floor King, who seem to have money to burn.'

'Peter,' said the little man earnestly, blowing a series of smoke-rings into the air, 'do not talk to me of these two wicked men. What advantage is it to them that they are well off for a few years, if they are to be miserable for all eternity? Do not despise your own honourable trade! Your father and grandfather were charcoal-burners, and did they not lead happy and good lives? I hope you have not come to me in search of a life of idleness!'

Peter had the grace to blush and, to tell the truth, he was a little frightened by the gravity of the little man's expression. 'No,' he replied. 'Well do I know, guardian of the forest, that idleness is the cause of all evils. But surely you can understand that I want to improve my position in life? After all, I could hardly be lower than a charcoal-burner! Glass-makers and raftsmen, clock-makers and woodmen are all far better off.'

'Careful, Peter, careful!' replied the little man. 'Pride often comes before a fall. What a strange race you humans are! Hardly ever is anyone satisfied with the position to which he has been born and bred. If you were a glass-maker you would want to be a wood-merchant, and if you were a wood-merchant you would want to be a forester or a banker. Well, all right, Peter, if you promise to work hard and conscientiously I will help you find something better. I offer three wishes to every Sunday's child who knows how to find me. The first two are free, but the third I can refuse if it is a foolish wish. Go ahead, then, and wish! But be sure to wish for something useful and good.'

'What an excellent Glass Manikin you are!' cried Peter. 'Well are you called the guardian of the treasure, for you have all treasures at your fingertips. Well then, what do I most want? To begin with, I want to dance better than the Dance-floor King and always to have as much money in my pocket as Big Ezekiel.'

'You fool!' thundered the little man. 'What an absurd wish – to ask for money for gambling and skill in dancing! Are you not ashamed of yourself, Peter? Well, you have one more free wish – see that you do not waste it!'

Peter scratched his head and said after some delay, 'All right. I wish for the most beautiful and most prosperous glass-works in the whole Black Forest, together with all the necessary implements and money to run it.'

'Anything else, Peter?' asked the little man anxiously.

'Well, I suppose I could do with a horse and carriage.'

'Oh, you idiotic boy!' cried the little man, and in his annoyance he flung his glass pipe against a pine tree, where it shattered into a thousand fragments. 'Horses? Carriages? Sense is what you should have wished for, plain common sense – not horses and carriages! All right, don't look so worried. Your second wish is not entirely bad, so we'll have to try to see that it does you no harm. A glass-works feeds its lord and master, and if only you had had the sense to see it you could have earned as many horses and carriages as you wanted.'

'But, sir,' said Peter, 'I still have one wish left. Could I not wish for sense and intelligence now, if you think they are so important?'

'No, no, Peter! You may be glad enough to have a spare wish up your sleeve. Off you go home now,' added the little man, taking a leather bag out of his pouch. 'Here are two thousand florins, and don't you dare to

come back here asking for more! If you do, I will hang
you from the highest pine tree, for that is my rule. Three
days ago the old fellow died who owned the big glass-
works in the lower forest. Go there tomorrow morning
and make an offer for the business. Work hard and honestly, and I will visit you from time to time to see that all
goes well, as you forgot to ask for common sense and have
none of your own. But I must warn you that your first
wish was wicked! Keep clear of the inn, Peter! It never
did anyone any good.' With these words the little fellow
shook Peter warmly by the hand, directed him on his
way and vanished into the undergrowth.

When Peter reached home he found his mother extremely worried on his account, but he soon cheered her
up by telling her how he had met a friend in the forest,

who had lent him enough money to set up in a more
prosperous and respectable kind of business than
charcoal-burning.

Although his mother had lived in the same little shack
for over thirty years and was as accustomed to black
faces around her as a miller's wife is used to white faces,
she was vain enough to despise her position the moment
Peter hinted at other possibilities. 'As mother of a glass-
maker I shall be rather better than an old charcoal wife,'
she said.

Peter wasted no time, and the glass-works was soon
his. To begin with he took a keen interest in the work. He
would wander into the factory in a leisurely fashion with
his hands in his pockets, look about him and speak to the
workmen, who were highly entertained by his stupid

questions. His greatest joy was to see glass being blown, and he often took the blow-pipe to his own lips and blew the most peculiar shapes. But before long he became bored with the glass-works and would visit it for only an hour a day, and then only every second day, and finally only once a week. Naturally his workmen did exactly as they pleased.

This was all the result of spending so much time at the inn. The Sunday after his return from the pine-tree hill he had gone to the inn, where he found Big Ezekiel and the Dance-floor King already ensconced behind enormous beer tankards, with a pile of money vulgarly displayed on the table. Quick as thought, Peter felt in his pocket to see if the Glass Manikin had kept his promise, and found that it was almost bursting with gold and silver coins. His legs jigged and twitched at the sound of the music, and as soon as the first dance was over he leapt up with his partner and took a position at the top of the dance beside the Dance-floor King, and if he leapt three feet in the air, Peter was sure to leap four, and if he showed off his clever and dainty steps, Peter amazed all the spectators with the brilliance of his own performance. There was no end to their astonishment when they heard that Peter had bought the glass-works, and when they saw him throw a handful of coins to the musicians every time he danced past them some thought that he must have found a treasure-hoard in the forest and others that he had inherited a fortune. But one and all paid great respect to him for no other reason than that he had money.

When Peter saw how highly people esteemed him, his pride and joy knew no bounds. He threw money about in handfuls and gave richly to the poor, for he himself had known how miserable poverty can be. The Dance-floor

King's arts were put to shame by the supernatural art of the new dancer, who was duly acclaimed whenever he displayed his skill. Not even the most desperate gamblers risked as much money as Peter did – but then, neither did they lose as much! This did not worry Peter in the slightest, for whenever he felt in his pocket he always found as much money as Big Ezekiel – who always had plenty. Indeed, as Ezekiel won most of Peter's money from him, the more he lost the more he had. If he handed over twenty or thirty florins to Ezekiel, he found an additional twenty or thirty florins in his own pocket.

Gradually he came to spend most of his time at the inn and became more notorious for his gambling than renowned for his dancing. His reputation in the neighbourhood grew most unenviable, even by the low standards set by such as Big Ezekiel, Skinny Willy and Dancing Joe. His glass factory fell into rack and ruin, and this was due to Peter's stupidity. He made as much glass as could be made, but he had not bought with the glass-works the secret of selling its products. Soon he had any amount of glass of first-quality, but he had not the faintest idea what to do with it. He finished by selling it off at half price to travelling merchants in order to pay the men's wages.

On the way home one evening he began to brood over the collapse of his fortunes, which even the excess of wine he had drunk could not conceal from him. Suddenly he became aware of someone walking beside him and looked round to see the Glass Manikin. Like all people who bring misfortune on themselves, Peter was only too eager to find someone else to blame. The Glass Manikin's reproachful look drove him to fury, for he had convinced himself that here was the root and cause of all his misfortunes. 'What's the use of my coach and horses now?' he exclaimed. 'What good does all my glass and the glass-works do me? I was better off as a charcoal-burner. Then at least I had no worries!'

'Indeed!' replied the Glass Manikin. 'Am I then to blame for your own stupidity? Is this your gratitude for my kindness? Is it my fault that you behaved like a fool? Did I not warn you to be careful how you wished? You lacked sense, Peter, plain common sense!'

'Plain common fiddlesticks!' cried Peter. 'I have as much sense as anyone in this forest, and I'll prove it to you!'

With these words he seized the manikin roughly by the scruff of the neck, shouting, 'Now I have you, guardian of the treasure, and you'll grant me my third wish here and now! Understand? I want two hundred thousand florins on the spot, in ready money, and a house, and – ow!' he cried, as the manikin turned into red-hot, molten glass in his hand, and slid from his grip amidst a shower of sparks. When the air cleared, the manikin was nowhere to be seen.

For many days Peter's swollen hand was a continual reminder of his stupidity and ingratitude. But after a while he managed to silence his conscience, and he said to himself, 'Well, even if my glass-works and everything else has to be sold, I at least have Big Ezekiel to fall back on. As long as he has money in his pocket I shall have plenty to live on.'

Yes, Peter, but what if he has no money? And so it was that soon afterwards the day of reckoning came. It was a Saturday night and the people already at the inn poked their heads out of the window to watch Peter arrive. 'Here comes Peter the gambler!' said one. 'So it is,' said another. 'Dancing Peter, the wealthy glass-maker!' And a third shook his head, saying, 'Wealthy he may have been, but now he is burdened by debts, and the bailiffs are to take over his property.'

Meanwhile Peter stepped out of his coach, greeted the people at the window, and called out, 'Good evening to you, landlord. Is there any word yet of Big Ezekiel?' And a deep voice called back, 'Come on in, Peter, I'm ready and waiting for you.' Peter felt in his pocket and was glad to find that Ezekiel must be well supplied with money, for his own pocket was full to bursting.

He sat down at the table and they began to play cards. Large sums of money changed hands, so large that soon all decent people put on their coats and went home. Only two men remained to watch, and after a time they too went away, saying, 'It's high time we were home. Our wives and children will be wondering what has happened to us.'

Peter persuaded Ezekiel to play on, though at first he was rather unwilling. 'All right,' said Ezekiel at last. 'Let me count my money and then we'll play dice. But it must be for five florins a throw – less than that is chicken-feed!' He pulled out his wallet and counted a hundred florins, and so Peter knew how much he had himself without bothering to count it.

Ezekiel had won most of the card games, but now everything seemed to go against him and Peter won throw after throw at the dice. Ezekiel grew more and more disconcerted and furious, until at length he took out his last five florins and placed them on the table, saying, 'One more throw, then, and even if I lose it there's no need to stop, Peter, for you can lend me money out of your winnings. An honest fellow like you is always willing to help a friend in need!'

'Of course,' replied Peter, 'borrow as much as you like. What about a hundred florins?' Peter had allowed his

success to go to his head. Ezekiel shook the dice and threw fifteen. 'Fine,' he declared. 'Let's see you beat that!' Peter threw an eighteen, and as the dice settled he heard a familiar gruff voice behind him say, 'That was the last!'

He looked round and saw the gigantic Dutch Michael towering above him, but it was clear that Big Ezekiel saw nothing, for he calmly asked Peter for a loan of ten florins. Half in a dream Peter dipped his hand into his pocket, but it was empty. He felt in his other pocket, but that too, was empty. He turned all his pockets inside out, but not a single penny was to be found. Only then did he remember his wish – that he should always have just as much money in his pockets as Big Ezekiel!

The landlord and Ezekiel looked at Peter in amazement as he searched and searched and found nothing. They simply could not believe that he had no money left. When at last they themselves had felt through all his pockets, they were livid with rage and accused Peter of being a sorcerer and of having wished all his winnings and his own money home to his house. Ezekiel swore he would tell everyone in the Black Forest what Peter had done, and the landlord threatened to place an accusation of sorcery before the city magistrates the very next morning. Then they fell on him in a rage, stripped him of his clothes and flung him out of the door.

Not a star shone in the sky, not a glimmer of moonlight, as Peter trudged sadly and wearily homeward, but there was just enough light for him to recognize the towering figure at his side.

'It's all up with you now, Peter!' said the figure at last. 'All your splendour is gone. I could have warned you of this that day on the pine-tree hill when you would have nothing to do with me, but ran to that mean Glass Manikin. But it is not too late even now! I am sorry for you Peter, truly! No one has ever regretted turning to me for help, and if you are not afraid you may find me on the pine-tree hill on Monday. Just call me, and I will come to you.'

Peter knew well enough who was talking to him, and a strange terror filled his breast. He made no reply, but ran home as fast as his legs would carry him.

When Peter went into his glass-works on Monday morning he found a crowd of people waiting, including the bailiff and his officers. The bailiff produced a heavy ledger, which contained the details of all Peter's creditors. 'Can you pay them? Yes or no?' demanded the bailiff. 'And be quick about it, for we have no time to waste,' he added, looking at Peter as he might have looked at a piece of dirt by the roadside. Peter gave up hope and confessed that he had nothing left. As the officers moved about his glass-works, assessing the value of everything, he thought that as the Glass Manikin had been no help to him he might as well try the big fellow. It was, after all, not far to the pine-tree hill. He ran to the hill as fast as if the bailiff and his officers had been hard on his heels. Barely had he gasped out, 'Dutch Michael! Dutch Michael!' than the huge raftsman stood in front of him, armed with his long staff.

'Aha!' said Michael with a laugh. 'I thought you would come! Have you managed to shake off your creditors? Well, well, your troubles are over now. Your present misery all stems from that little glass fellow, as I told you. But come with me to my house, and I am sure we shall be able to do business together.'

Business? thought Peter. What can he want from me, when I am quite penniless? What have I to offer him?

They crossed a little wooded spur and descended steeply into a precipitous ravine, at the foot of which lay Dutch Michael's house. It seemed quite an ordinary house, differing from other houses only in its loneliness and distance from other human habitation. He followed Dutch Michael inside and sat down at the table, while Michael went to fetch glasses and a flagon of wine. A big glassful was poured out for each of them, and they began to talk. Michael had a great many exciting stories to tell of the pleasures of life, of foreign countries, beautiful cities and rivers, not to mention beautiful women. Peter sat enthralled, which was exactly what Dutch Michael wanted.

'You have plenty of courage,' he said, 'and great physical strength, and you could do great things, were it not for the promptings of your stupid heart. Why should any sensible person worry about things like honour or other people's misfortunes? What was it that hurt you when the bailiffs came to throw you out of your house and glass-works? Tell me now, what was it?'

'My heart,' said Peter, pressing his hand to his breast, for it felt as if his heart was jumping about inside him, in sudden alarm.

'Don't take it amiss,' continued Michael, 'but you have thrown away a vast amount of money to beggars and other riff-raff. What do you think drove you to dip deep into your own pocket whenever a beggar stretched out his dirty ragged hat towards you? Your heart, once again, your heart. To speak truly, you took the plight of these beggar-folk too much to heart.'

'But how can I prevent my heart troubling me in this way? I do my best to suppress it, but it goes on beating and makes me miserable.'

'Of course, you can do nothing about it,' replied Michael with a laugh. 'But give me the beating heart and you'll see how well you manage without it.'

'Give you my heart!' exclaimed Peter in horror. 'I should die on the spot! How could I give you my heart?'

'Yes, indeed you would die if a surgeon were to operate on you and remove your heart, but my method is quite different. Come next door and see for yourself.'

With these words he got to his feet and showed Peter into the next room, where an astounding sight met his eyes. Wooden shelves lined the walls, and on them stood row upon row of glass jars, filled with transparent fluid, and in each of these jars lay a pulsating human heart. Each jar had a label with a name written on it, and

235

Peter was curious enough to read several of them. Here was the heart of a well-known but heartily disliked magistrate; there was Big Ezekiel's heart; there was the Dance-floor King's, and there, even the chief forester's heart. There were six hearts belonging to grain merchants, eight belonging to recruiting officers, three belonging to money-lenders – in short, it was a collection of the hearts of all the most distinguished and important people for fifty miles around.

'Just look!' said Michael. 'All these people have laid aside the fears and sorrows of ordinary life. Not one of these hearts affects its owner one way or the other, and their owners are all perfectly happy without them.'

'But what do they carry in their breasts in place of their hearts?' asked Peter, who was giddy with what he had seen.

'This,' replied Michael, reaching into a pigeon-hole, and handed him a heart of stone!

'This?' echoed Peter, unable to suppress a shudder. 'A marble heart? But surely, Dutch Michael, it must feel very cold in one's breast?'

'Of course it does,' was the warm reply. 'Pleasantly cool and calm. Why should the heart be warm? The warmth is no use to you in winter. A good glass of brandy will do more to warm you than a warm heart. And in summer, when the weather is hot and sultry, you have no idea how cooling it is to have a cold stone heart.'

'Is this all you have to offer me?' asked Peter, sulkily. 'I came to you hoping for money, and you offer me a stone!'

'Well, I was thinking of a hundred thousand florins to begin with,' said Michael. 'If you use it cleverly, you can soon be a millionaire.'

'A hundred thousand!' cried Peter, hardly believing

his ears. 'Stop beating away so violently inside me!' he said to his heart. 'Very well, Michael. Give me the stone and the money, and you are welcome to my troublesome heart.'

'I thought you would see sense,' said Michael with a laugh. 'Come, let's have another drink while I count out the money.'

So they sat down again at the table and drank glass after glass of wine, until Peter fell into a deep sleep.

He was awakened by the loud trumpeting of a posthorn, and found himself sitting in a fine coach travelling along a broad highway, and as he sat up to look round him he saw the faint outline of the blue hills of the Black Forest fading into the distance behind him. At first he thought he must be dreaming, for even his clothes were different from the ones he had been wearing, but he remembered everything so clearly that at length he gave up wondering how the change had come about and accepted the fact that he was alive and well.

To begin with, he was puzzled that he felt no sorrow at leaving the hills of home behind him for the first time, the land where he had been born and bred. Not even the thought of his old mother, left helpless and penniless, brought a tear to his eye. It seemed of no great importance. 'I understand,' he said on reflection. 'Tears and sighs, homesickness and vain regrets, sadness and sorrow all come from the heart, and Dutch Michael has given me a heart of cold stone instead.'

For two years he travelled about in his fine coach, surveying the buildings and countryside that passed on either side and living in the best inns wherever he stopped. He made a point of seeing all the most beautiful places in each city he visited, but nothing pleased him, for he was blind and deaf to beauty of any sort. Beautiful pictures, fine buildings, sublime music, even the most graceful dancing meant nothing to him now.

No joy remained for him but the pleasure of eating and drinking, and so the days passed in travelling aimlessly from one city to another, eating and drinking to pass the time, and sleeping out of boredom.

When he passed through Strassburg and glimpsed the dark forests of his homeland, when he saw for the first time in two years the honest, kindly faces of the people of the Black Forest, when he once again heard the familiar accents of his own folk, he felt a sudden new vigour in his limbs and fire in his blood, and he did not know whether to laugh or cry, but – how could he be so stupid! he had a stone heart. And stones are dead; they can neither laugh nor cry.

His first visit was to Dutch Michael, who gave him a friendly welcome. 'Well, Michael,' said Peter, 'I have done all the travelling I want to do and have seen all I want to see, but I must confess I was bored with it all. This stone thing of yours that I carry about with me gives me complete protection from many things. I am never angry or sad, but neither am I ever happy, and I seem to be only half alive. Could you not put just a little feeling into your stone heart or, better still, give me my old heart back again? In twenty-five years I had become used to it, and even if it did cause me to do silly things sometimes it was at least a live and happy heart.'

'When you are dead, Peter,' replied Dutch Michael, with a harsh and bitter laugh, 'you shall have your own soft, emotional heart back again, and then you will be able to feel joys and sorrows. But here on earth it can never again be yours! Settle down somewhere in the forest, build yourself a house, find yourself a bride and set to work to build up a fortune. You were bored only because you had nothing to do with it.' Peter saw the truth of this argument and decided to pursue the acquisition of more and more wealth. Michael gave him a further hundred thousand florins to be going on with, and they parted the best of friends.

The news travelled through the Black Forest like wildfire that Peter the charcoal-burner was home again, richer than ever. When he had been a dirty but honest charcoal-burner, he had been thrown out of the inn, but now he was welcomed back with open arms, for he clearly had plenty of money. The landlord and others showed great interest in his travels, and before long he was again playing cards and dice for money with Big Ezekiel, and his credit stood as high as ever.

This time there was no question of a glass-works. Peter entered the timber trade, but this was only for the sake of appearances. His real business was dealing in grain and money. After a while half the people in the Black Forest were in debt to him, for he lent money only at ten per cent interest and sold corn for three times its normal price to poor people who were unable to pay at once. He struck up a friendship with the magistrate, and if Herr Peter Munk was not paid his dues on the dot, the bailiff and his officers would turn the poor debtors out into the forest – father, mother and children.

To begin with this caused the wealthy Peter much annoyance, for the poor people he had ruined crowded round his door – the men begging more time to pay, the women hoping to melt his hard heart, and the starving children begging for a crust of bread. But this caterwauling, as he called it, came to an abrupt stop when he bought a couple of powerful mastiffs.

His greatest source of annoyance was 'the old woman'. This was none other than Frau Munk, Peter's mother. Two years previously she had been driven out of a house and home when the property had been sold, and her son, when he returned as a rich man, paid not the slightest attention to her. From time to time she would hobble along to his house, supported by her stick, for she was old and shaky on her feet. She no longer dared to go inside the house, for he had driven her away once already, but it hurt her to have to live on other people's charity, when her own son could so easily have given her a carefree and comfortable old age, without noticing the cost. But Peter's heart was unmoved by the suffering which showed only too plainly on her pale familiar features, nor did the decrepit figure, the limp outstretched hand and the pathetic, beseeching looks give him the slightest pang of pity or remorse. When she knocked at the door on Saturdays, he would take a florin from his pocket with an ill grace and order a servant to take it out to the old woman. He could hear her trembling voice outside, thanking him and wishing him joy. He could hear her coughing as she shuffled away from the door, but all he thought was that he had wasted a florin.

At last Peter took it into his head to get married. He knew very well that every father in the Black Forest would willingly have given him his daughter because of his great wealth, but he was hard to please and wanted to be praised by his prospective father-in-law for his intelligence! So he rode all over the forest, inspecting the beautiful girls of the district, but not one of them did he find beautiful enough. At last, after he had searched in vain through every dance-floor, he heard that the most virtuous and most beautiful girl in the whole Black Forest was the daughter of a poor woodman. He made up his mind on the spot that he would marry the girl, so he rode straight to the hut where she lived.

Fair Lisbeth's father was amazed when he realized that this was the rich Herr Peter Munk about whom he had heard so much, and still more amazed when Peter announced his desire to become his son-in-law. It did not take him long to make up his mind, for he was convinced that the marriage would mean an end to his poverty, and he agreed without even asking the fair Lisbeth what she felt about it. But she was such an obedient daughter that she obeyed her father without demur, and became Frau Peter Munk.

But the poor girl was soon disillusioned, for her marriage brought her not a moment's happiness. Nothing she did in the house pleased Peter, and he was for ever grumbling and finding fault with her. She was always sorry for the poor, and as her husband was so well off she could see no harm in giving a penny to an old beggar-woman in rags. But Peter was furious when he saw her do it, and shouted at her in a rage, 'Why are you squandering my money on beggars and ragamuffins! Have you any money of your own, that you give it away so freely? Let me catch you at it once more and you shall feel my hand!'

Fair Lisbeth went to her room and wept bitterly, for she could not understand her husband's meanness. A thousand times she wished she could be back in her father's little hut, in spite of its poverty. After this, whenever she sat at the door and a beggar passed by, cap in hand, she closed her eyes so that she should not see the poor fellow's misery and clenched her fists tightly in case she should dip into her pocket involuntarily to bring out a penny. So it came about that Lisbeth was scorned throughout the forest, and was said to be even more miserly than her husband.

One day Lisbeth sat spinning on the doorstep,

humming a gay tune, for the sun was shining and Peter had ridden away for the day. Suddenly a little old man appeared, wizened and bent, carrying a large, heavy sack on his back; she could hear him panting and gasping from quite a long way off. Lisbeth was full of sympathy, well knowing that such an old man should not have to carry such a heavy burden.

Meanwhile the old man stumbled and panted along under his load until he was opposite the door, where he all but collapsed. 'Have pity, kind lady,' implored the little old man, 'and let me have a sip of water. I cannot go a step further. I am quite exhausted.'

'You ought not to be carrying a load like that at your age,' said Lisbeth.

'That's easy to say,' he replied, 'but I haven't a penny to my name and I must earn my living somehow, and

this is the only work I can do. A rich woman like you can have no idea what it is like to be poor! Never mind, a sip of cool water will do me a world of good in this heat.'

Lisbeth hurried into the house, took a jug from the shelf and filled it with water; but when she turned and saw the poor old man sitting miserably on his sack she was overwhelmed with pity, set the jug of water aside and filled a glass with wine. After all, her husband was away from home, so what harm could there possibly be in giving the old man some wine and a slice of good rye bread? 'Here you are,' she said. 'A sip of wine will do you more good than water, but do not drink it too quickly and eat the bread with it.'

The little old man was overcome with gratitude. 'I am old,' he said, 'and have travelled far, but I have never met anyone so kind or so beautiful. Such generosity will surely be rewarded.'

'Indeed it will!' cried a harsh, grating voice. 'And she shall have her reward here and now!' They turned round, and there stood Peter, his face crimson with fury.

'So you wait till my back is turned, and give away my best wine to beggar-folk,' he screamed, 'and one of my best glasses to the rabble of the streets! Here, then, is your reward!' Lisbeth threw herself on her knees and begged for mercy, but the stone heart knew no pity. Peter turned his whip and struck her so violently on the forehead with the ebony handle that she fell lifeless into the old man's arms. As soon as he saw what he had done Peter regretted it and bent over the body to see if there was any sign of life, but the old man said in a familiar voice, 'Do not bother, Peter the charcoal-burner. She was the fairest flower that ever bloomed in the Black Forest, and you have trampled her underfoot. She will never bloom again.'

Peter turned white as a sheet when he heard the voice. 'So it's you, guardian of the treasure? Well, what's done is done, and there is no help for it. I hope you are not going to let the magistrates know about this?'

'Miserable wretch!' replied the Glass Manikin.'What good would it do me to send your mortal husk to the gallows? No, you need fear no earthly court of law, but how will you defend yourself before God? For you have sold your immortal soul to the Devil.'

'Well, even if I have sold my heart,' cried Peter, 'it is only you and your deceitful gifts that are to blame! It is you who ruined me and drove me to seek help from another. On you lies the whole responsibility.' But scarcely had the words left his lips than the Glass Manikin began to swell to an enormous size, till his eyes were as big as soup plates and his mouth like a fiery furnace, with flames darting from it. Peter flung himself on his knees, and even his stone heart did not prevent him quivering like an aspen-tree in every limb. With vulture's claws the spirit of the forest gripped him by the scruff of the neck and shook him, spun him round and round like a whirlwind and flung him to the ground with such force that all his ribs seemed to crack. 'Worm!' he cried in a voice of thunder. 'I could crush you to pulp if I wanted, for you have committed an outrage against the lord of the forest. But for the sake of this dead woman, I give you eight days' grace!'

Not till it was growing dark did some passers-by notice the rich Peter Munk lying on the ground. They turned him over and over to see if he was still breathing, but for a long time it looked as if he were dead. At last one of them went into the house, brought out some water and sprinkled it over Peter's face. A deep sigh came from the prostrate Peter, then a groan, and his eyes flickered open. He asked for Lisbeth, but no one had seen her. He thanked the man for his help and crept into his house, where he searched in vain for his wife. He had hoped it was all a terrible dream, but found it grim reality. Strange thoughts crowded in on him in his loneliness. He was afraid of nothing, for his heart was cold and hard, but when he thought of his wife's death he could hardly help thinking of his own, and of the heavy burden he would take with him when he faced the last judgement – the tears of the poor, the curses of the thousands he had wronged, the despair of his aged mother and, worst of all, the blood of the fair Lisbeth. He could not even answer the poor girl's father if he came and asked for his daughter. How, then, would he be able to answer the Marker of Heaven and earth?

Night after night he was tormented by vivid dreams, which all ended with the same soft voice calling, 'Peter, Peter, what you need is a warmer heart!' This always woke him up, but then he would close his eyes quickly and bury himself beneath the bedclothes, for it was his wife Lisbeth's voice giving him this warning. One day he went to the inn to drown his sorrows in drink, and there he met Big Ezekiel. They chatted together about this and that – about the fine warm weather, about war, about taxes and finally about death and how it was that so many people died suddenly and without warning. Peter asked Ezekiel if he believed in a life after death, and Ezekiel said he was sure that when a man's body was buried his soul either went up to heaven or down to hell.

'Do they bury a man's heart with his body?' asked Peter anxiously.

'Yes, of course,' replied Big Ezekiel.

'What happens, then, if he no longer possesses his heart?' continued Peter.

245

The blood drained from Ezekiel's face. 'What do you mean by that?' he asked through clenched teeth. 'Are you trying to make a fool of me? Are you implying that I have no heart?'

'Of course you have,' replied Peter, 'as hard as stone!'

Ezekiel was thunderstruck. He looked round to make sure that no one was listening. 'What do you know about it?' he whispered hoarsely. 'Or is your own heart no longer beating?'

'No, it is no longer beating,' sighed Peter, 'at any rate not here in my breast. But, tell me, now that you know what I am talking about, what do you think will happen to our hearts when we die?'

'Nothing good, I'm sure of that,' replied Ezekiel. 'I once asked a schoolmaster about it, and he assured me that our hearts are all weighed when we die, to see which ones are heaviest with sins. The light ones rise up to heaven and the heavy ones sink down. I reckon our stones will be a fair weight.'

'I'm afraid so,' said Peter. 'It's a dreadful thought. I want to feel joy and sorrow, and it troubles me that I cannot.'

That night Peter was wakened five or six times with the soft, gentle voice murmuring in his ear, 'Peter, find yourself a warmer heart!' He could feel no regret at having murdered her, but when he told the servants that she was away on a journey he realized how hollow and unconvincing it sounded.

So things went on for six days, and night after night he heard the same soft, persistent voice. The Glass Manikin's threat was ever present in his mind, till he could think of nothing else. At the crack of dawn on the seventh morning he leapt out of bed, crying, 'All right,

I'll do my best to find a warmer heart, for this cold stone has made life harsh and meaningless.' He dressed in his best clothes, mounted his horse, and set out for the pine-tree hill.

He dismounted when the hill rose in front of him and the pines became dense, tied his horse to a tree and went the rest of the way on foot to the tall pine tree on the summit, where he recited:

> 'Guardian of the forest treasure,
> Watchman here for many a year,
> Do your utmost for my pleasure,
> To Sunday's child you must appear.'

Out came the Glass Manikin, but this time he had lost his kindly smile and was sunk in a deep melancholy. He was wearing a suit of black glass with a black ribbon wound round his hat, and there was no need to ask for whom he was mourning.

'What do you want from me, Peter Munk?' he asked.

'I still have one wish left, guardian of the treasure,' replied Peter, keeping his eyes downcast.

'Yet I can refuse it, if it is foolish,' replied the forest spirit. 'However, let me hear what you want!'

'Take away this dead stone and give me my living heart,' said Peter.

'Why come to me?' asked the little man. 'Am I Dutch Michael, who trades in money and cold stones? No, you must ask him for your heart.'

'It is no use!' replied Peter sadly. 'He will never part with it.'

'Wicked though you are, I am sorry for you,' said the little man, after a moment's thought. 'As your wish is in no way a foolish one, I cannot, at any rate, refuse my

247

help. I suppose you realize that no power on earth can force Michael to give up your heart? But cunning may do what force cannot, and this may not be so difficult as you might think, for Michael is a stupid fellow, however high an opinion he may have of himself. Here is what you must do.'

He whispered a few hurried words into Peter's ear and gave him a tiny cross of pure glass. 'Once you have your heart,' he added, 'come back here to me.'

Peter took the little cross, carefully memorized his instructions and went on towards Dutch Michael's dwelling. He called him three times by name, and suddenly the giant appeared before him.

'I hear you have killed your wife!' cried Michael with a terrible laugh. 'You were quite right. She was a menace to your security, giving away all your money to beggarfolk. But I suppose this means you will have to go abroad for a time, for there will certainly be questions asked when she fails to return. You need some money for the journey?'

'That's right,' replied Peter, 'and plenty of it, for it is a long way to America.'

Michael led the way into the house and opened a huge chest full of gold. He lifted several bags of gold from it on to the table, and as he was counting it out, Peter said, 'You're an old devil, Michael, spinning me that yarn about putting a stone in my breast and keeping my heart here!'

'It is quite true,' declared Michael. 'Do you feel your heart? Is it not as cold as ice? Are you afraid of anything? Can you repent of anything you have done?'

'Perhaps not,' said Peter, 'but it's here in my breast all the same. Ezekiel still has his heart, too.'

Michael was growing angry. 'But I assure you,' he cried, 'your heart and Ezekiel's, and the hearts of all those rich people who have had dealings with me are here in my room.'

'Oh no, no, no!' laughed Peter. 'You cannot fool me twice! Try telling that story to a child, if you like! You forget that I have seen something of the world. Do you think I cannot recognize wax hearts when I see them? You're a clever fellow, I don't deny it, but do not claim you can conjure men's hearts out of their bodies. Oh no, you cannot expect me to believe that!'

Michael was filled with rage and flung open the door. 'Come on in then,' he cried, 'and read this label. Is this not Peter Munk's heart? See it twitching? Could a wax heart twitch like that?'

'Oh, it's clever enough, I grant you,' said Peter. 'But it is wax all the same. My heart is here, in my breast. There is no magic about it!'

'I'll prove it to you,' shouted Michael in a fury. 'Come, see what your real heart feels like.'

He took the warm, pulsating heart from its jar, ripped open Peter's jacket and tore the cold stone heart from his breast. Then he laid the real heart carefully in its place, and at once Peter felt it beating and was filled with an overwhelming joy.

'Well, how does it feel?' laughed Michael.

'Indeed,' replied Peter, as he carefully took his glass cross from his pocket, 'I think you must have been right after all. I would hardly have believed it possible!'

'Well, I am glad you are convinced,' said Michael. 'Come, then. Let me replace your stone heart.'

'Come, come, Michael!' cried Peter, taking a step back and holding up the glass cross. 'Mice are caught by

249

cheese, and this time you are the mouse.' And he began to pray as he had never prayed before.

Suddenly Michael began to shrink, until he writhed on the ground like a worm, whining and groaning. At the same time all the hearts in the room began to twitch and beat violently, trying to escape from their glass jars, so that it sounded like a clockmaker's work-shop. Peter had never been so frightened in his life, and he fled from the dreadful house. Up the steep ravine he clambered, scaling the cliffs at the top without daring to look down, for by this time Dutch Michael had struggled to his feet and was hurling curses and threats from below. On and on he ran towards the pine-tree hill, while thunder crashed overhead and javelins of lightning hurtled through the trees all around. Trees were shattered to right and left of him, but by a miracle he reached the Glass Manikin's terrain unscathed.

His heart beat for the sheer joy of beating. But suddenly he remembered all he had done; how he had wantonly destroyed and harmed all those with whom he had come in contact, just as the storm had shattered the pine forest behind him. He thought of his beautiful wife Lisbeth, struck down through greed and ill-temper. He saw himself despised by all men. His heart was full, and tears were streaming down his cheeks when he reached the great pine tree where the Glass Manikin was waiting, looking very much happier than when Peter had left him.

'Well, Peter the charcoal-burner,' he said, 'what are you crying for? Could you not get your heart back?'

'Alas!' cried Peter. 'When I had my cold stone heart I never cried. My eyes were as dry as the parched Sahara. But now it almost breaks my old heart to think what I have done! I have driven my debtors to despair and poverty, I have set the dogs on the poor and the sick and the elderly, and – you of all people should know how my whip fell on her fair brow!'

'You were a great sinner, Peter,' said the little man. 'You were ruined by money and idleness. Your heart turned to stone and knew neither joy nor sorrow, neither pity nor remorse. But true repentance can work miracles, and perhaps I might do something for you yet if only I could be sure that you were truly penitent.'

'There's nothing more I want,' replied Peter, sinking his head sadly on to his knees. 'What is there to live for? Will anyone ever speak to me again? My mother will never forgive my conduct, even if she has survived my ill-treatment of her! As for Lisbeth, my beautiful wife! No, guardian of the treasure, strike me dead, I beg you, lest I cause any more suffering.'

'All right,' replied the little man, 'if that is what you want, perhaps you are right. I will fetch my axe.' Calmly he knocked the ashes out of his glass pipe and put it in his pocket. Slowly he stood up and went round behind the great pine tree. Peter sat miserably in the grass, crying his heart out, and waited patiently for the fatal blow. After a few moments he heard soft footsteps in the grass behind him, and thought that now the axe would fall.

'Look round, Peter Munk!' cried the little man. Peter wiped his eyes on his sleeve, looked round and saw his mother and Lisbeth his wife, smiling towards him. He leapt to his feet, hardly daring to believe his eyes. 'Is it really you, Lisbeth? Didn't you die? And you, dear Mother, can you ever forgive me?'

'Of course they forgive you,' said the little man, 'because you are truly repentant. Try to forget what has happened, and go back to your father's hut to carry on the noble trade of charcoal-burning. If you do it well, if you are persevering and honest in your dealings, you will be more highly respected than if you possessed all the gold in the world.'

All three praised and blessed the manikin, and then made their way home.

Peter was neither surprised nor disappointed to find that his magnificent house had been struck by lightning and had burned to the ground with all his treasures. But he was not saddened by his loss. What does it matter? he thought. It is not far to my father's hut.

But what a surprise awaited them when they reached the hut, for they found it changed into a fine house – not big, but simple and practical, and much more convenient than the big house with its numerous servants had been.

'This is the work of the Glass Manikin,' said Peter. 'How kind and thoughtful of him!' 'How beautiful and how perfect!' cried Lisbeth.

From that time on, Peter worked hard and honestly at his father's trade. He was satisfied with what he had, and in time he became prosperous through his own efforts and was highly respected in the community. His warm heart never failed to prompt him in the service of others, and he was well liked by everyone with whom he came in contact. He never quarrelled with Lisbeth, he looked after his mother tenderly and gave willingly to all the poor and needy who came to him for help. When Lisbeth gave birth to a fine baby boy, he took his child to the top of the pine-tree hill and said his piece – but the Glass Manikin did not appear. 'Guardian of the treasure!' cried Peter. 'Hear me! I have come to ask you to be my son's godfather.' But there was no reply, only a slight

gust of wind which rustled through the trees and threw six fir-cones at his feet. 'Very well,' sighed Peter. 'Since you will not show yourself I will take these as a souvenir,' and he put the fir-cones in his pocket and returned home.

That evening his mother was hanging up his jacket in the wardrobe when she felt something bulky in the pockets. She looked to see what it was and found six little bags of gold coins. It was the Glass Manikin's gift to little Peter.

They lived quietly and happily for many a long year, and often – even when he was old, with grey hair – Peter would declare, 'It is far better to be happy with few possessions than to have all the money in the world and a cold heart.'

Dear Parents

If you have given your child the first, the second and now the third big story-book, you have shown that you are thinking of his mental and spiritual needs as well as his physical ones. A child will derive more pleasure from books if they are properly suited to his age, and that is why I have offered you a varied selection of stories from all over the world, sorted into three different steps or age-groups.

It is unfortunately true that a great many parents shirk the responsibility of guiding their children's reading once they are past the first years of early childhood, in the belief that young children are quite capable of choosing their own reading matter. However safe such an attitude may have been in the past, it is now no longer valid. Think for a moment of the irresponsible people who make a profit out of comics, horror stories, crime stories, stories of war and hatred – regardless of the irreparable damage such appalling "literature" can do to the delicate and tender plant which is the child's spiritual and intellectual development.

I beg and implore you to pay due attention to what your child reads. He needs protection from all that is bad in current writing for the young. For as long as you can afford it, you must make sure that he has ready access to good books.

If you are uncertain what books are suitable for your child, there are plenty of qualified people who are ready and willing to advise you. Do not hesitate to seek their help. Above all, make sure that your child has a good bookcase of his own, filled with plenty of good books. If your child's thirst for reading matter outgrows your purse, you can always fall back on the public libraries, nearly all of which have children's rooms with qualified librarians in charge.

Remember, however, that you must set a good example yourself. Lay aside the newspaper or the latest glossy magazine, and let your child see you absorbed in your book. Sad indeed is the home where the family cannot gather quietly round the fire with their books. They do not know what they are missing!

RICHARD BAMBERGER